DRAGONFIRE

DRAGONFIRE

Bill Pronzini

PaperJacks LTD.

TORONTO   NEW YORK

PaperJacks

DRAGONFIRE

PaperJacks LTD

330 STEELCASE RD. E., MARKHAM, ONT. L3R 2M1
210 FIFTH AVE., NEW YORK, N.Y. 10010

PaperJacks edition published July 1987

ISBN 0-7701-0503-3
Printed in the USA

This one is for Sharon McCone, the best of the lady private eyes, and for her creator, Marcia Muller

ONE

Welcome to hard times . . .

Sunday afternoon, mid-August. Eberhardt and I were sitting in the backyard of his house in Noe Valley, drinking beer and getting a little tight. It was a nice day— bright sunlight, warm, just a hint of breeze. The smell of burning charcoal was in the air; Eb had started the coals in the brick barbecue pit he'd built some years back and we were going to have steaks pretty soon. In one of the other yards beyond his fence, somebody was mowing his lawn; you could hear the faint ratchety whir of a hand-powered mower.

It was all nice and pleasant: one of those lazy days of summer, a Sunday rite like thousands of others in San Francisco. The only problem with it was, neither of us was enjoying it. Eberhardt's wife Dana had left him for another man three months ago, after nearly three decades of marriage, and he was lonely and bitter and rattled around in his house like a marble in a box. And I was even worse off. I had also lost a woman I loved, for different reasons—or it seemed I'd lost her from all indications the past month. Eberhardt, at least, had his job—he was a lieutenant on the San Francisco cops—and could bury himself in his work. But I no longer had mine. That was something else I'd lost a month ago: the only profession I had had for the past thirty years. My private investigator's license had been sus-

[1]

pended indefinitely by the State Board of Licenses, on recommendation of the chief of police.

We had been sitting there guzzling beer for about three hours. Eberhardt had invited me over and I'd accepted for similar reasons; misery loves company and it was always easier to drown your sorrows with a friend and fellow sufferer. Neither of us had mentioned our respective troubles so far, but I knew that wasn't going to last. And it didn't.

Eberhardt was over poking around in the barbecue pit. When he came back and plunked himself down again in his chaise longue he said, "Another twenty minutes should do it." Then he drank some beer and said, "You seen Kerry lately?"

"Yeah, I saw her. Last week."

"How'd it go?"

"Strained," I said. "We had lunch in a place out at China Basin."

"So what did she say?"

"She still hasn't made up her mind. Hasn't had enough time yet. My situation isn't making it any easier for her, I guess."

"She still getting flack from her old man?"

"She didn't say. But you can bet she is; he's a relentless bugger, Wade is."

"When're you seeing her again?"

"Who knows?"

"You talking to her regularly?"

"Once or twice a week."

"You call or does she?"

"She does, for the most part," I said. "I don't want to put any more pressure on her. She's worried about me so she calls to find out how I'm holding up."

"How are you holding up?"

"Okay. Getting through."

We both fell silent. I watched him load tobacco into one of his pipes, a thing carved in the shape of a head that he

[2]

had taken a liking to. The talk about Kerry made memories of her lie heavy on my mind. I'd met her back in May, at a pulp writers' convention that had evolved into a double homicide case; her parents, Cybil and Ivan Wade, were both ex-pulp writers. We had established both an emotional and physical rapport almost immediately, and I'd fallen in love with her, and not long after that I'd asked her to marry me. That was when the problems started. Her father, Ivan the Terrible, as I called him, thought I was too old for her because I was fifty-three and she was thirty-eight; he didn't like the fact that I was a private detective and he didn't like me. So he'd started pressuring her. And then I'd started pressuring her too, and it became a kind of tug-of-war with Kerry in the middle.

It had all come to a head during a crazy week in July—the worst week of my life because it contained a whole slew of other events that combined to bring about the suspension of my investigator's license. I developed a stupid streak of jealousy and all but accused Kerry of fooling around with one of the owners of the advertising agency where she worked; we'd had words about that. Then her old man showed up at my flat and I had words with him too, angry words, and wound up threatening him and throwing him out. Kerry hadn't liked that, either.

Toward the end of that week we'd gone out to dinner, and the evening degenerated into a fight. She said we didn't know each other as well as we thought we did; she said I had old-fashioned macho tendencies and couldn't deal with a relationship unless it was on my terms; she said that maybe I wanted her just because her parents were pulp writers and the pulps were a central part of my life. A few days later she'd come to my office on Drumm Street and told me she needed time to make up her mind, a sense of freedom, and it would be better if we didn't see each other for a while. That had more or less finished things. In the month since that day, I had spoken to her maybe eight times on the phone and seen her twice. And it just wasn't the same between us; it wasn't even close. I did not see how it could ever be again.

Eberhardt had his pipe going and was making fierce sucking noises on the stem. His face, with its odd mix of angles and blunt planes, had a dark broody look. He seemed to be in the same kind of grim mood I was in today.

I said, "How're things with you, Eb?"

"Lousy. Too much on my mind."

"Heavy work load?"

"Yeah. I hate my goddamn job sometimes. It's a hell of a thing being a cop, you know that?"

"Somebody's got to do it. And you're one of the best."

"Am I? I don't know about that."

"Anything wrong?"

He gave me a look. "Why do you think anything's wrong?"

"I don't think it. I was just asking."

"Well, I don't want to talk about it."

"All right. Sure."

He scowled at his pipe and put it down. "Then there's Dana," he said. "My ever-loving whore of a wife."

"She's not a whore, Eb."

"The hell she's not. Don't tell me about whores; I know all about whores."

"Have you talked to her recently?"

"Not in weeks. Last time she called, she wanted a couple of things—furniture for her new apartment. She didn't even ask me how I was."

"Where's she living?"

"She wouldn't tell me. Wouldn't give me her phone number, either."

"You think she's living alone?"

"Hell, no. Moved in somewhere with her boyfriend."

"You ever find out who he is?"

"No. And I hope I never do. If I did . . ."

"What?"

"I don't know what. Shoot the bastard, maybe. Her too. Blow both of them away."

"Come on, Eb."

"You think I'm kidding?"

"You've been a cop too long for a thing like that."

"Maybe. Maybe not. You don't know what I'm liable to do; neither do I. Bastards like that deserve to get shot. So do whores. Whores are better off dead anyway. Who cares about a damned whore?"

I didn't say anything; the subject was depressing and I wanted to get off it. I finished my beer. "You ready for another one of these?"

"Yeah."

I went into the kitchen and got two more cans out of the refrigerator. When I came back out he was at the barbecue pit again, poking the charcoal around; most of the briquettes were already glowing and white. I gave him his fresh beer and wandered over and leaned against his board fence, in the shade of a Japanese elm. I was feeling the effects of the beer, but it wasn't a good kind of high; it made me melancholy and added to the lost, empty, aimless state I had been mired in for the past month.

I no longer had any purpose in life, no reason for my existence. It wasn't a suicidal frame of mind; just an emptiness, a vacuum in which I seemed to be drifting. If I'd had Kerry, if things had been the way they were for us in the beginning, I could have weathered the suspension and found a way to go on. As it was I had nothing to hang on to, no enthusiasm for anything. It was as if all meaning had been cut out of me and the operation had turned me into an emotional vegetable.

At the barbecue Eberhardt said, "You got any job prospects lined up yet?"

"No. I haven't been looking."

"Why not?"

"What the hell am I going to do, Eb? Being an investigator is the only thing I'm qualified for."

"There must be something else you can do."

"Sure. Wash dishes, run errands, become a clerk in a cigar store. I'm too damned old for anything like that."

"You got to eat."

"I still have some savings left."

"Sure. How much?"

"Enough to last me another month."

"Then what?"

"I don't know. I'll worry about that when the time comes."

"You could sell off some of those pulps of yours."

"Last resort," I said. "If it gets to that I might as well throw in the towel."

He put down the poker he'd been using and came over to stand next to me at the fence. "You give up your office yet?"

"Not yet. Rent's paid until the end of this month."

"What about the furniture and stuff?"

"I guess I'll sell it. Or give it away to the Salvation Army. I can't afford to put it into storage, that's for sure. And even if I could, why bother? I'll never need office furniture again."

"You don't know that," he said. "The State Board promised a review in six months, didn't they?"

"Sure. A review. Even if they lift the suspension, which they won't, how do I pick up the pieces? All my steady clients are gone and they wouldn't come back. And where do I get new ones? Nobody's going to want to hire a private detective who's had his license suspended and been raked over the media coals the way I was."

"People forget. New people come into the city all the time. You could build up business again."

"Maybe. But I'd starve to death in the meantime."

"You're going to starve as it is."

"Look, forget it. It's not going to happen anyway. I'll never be given a license again in California."

"You could try getting one in another state."

"With this hanging over me here? They'd turn me down flat, you know that, no matter where I went."

"It's still worth a try."

"So maybe I will," I said, but I knew I wouldn't. I could not afford to move somewhere else and start over; it just wasn't in me even if I could swing it.

Eberhardt finished half of his beer; his eyes were starting to take on a faintly glassy sheen. "What're you doing with your days, if you're not out looking for work?"

"Not much. Reading, moping around, drinking beer."

"I guess I know all about that."

"Yeah."

"Yeah," he agreed. He tilted the can to his mouth again.

A maudlin indignation seemed to be creeping through me. I said, "It's so goddamned unfair, Eb. What the hell did I do to deserve a suspension? Got mixed up in some things that weren't my fault, did my job in each case, resolved them all. They took away my license because I'm good at what I do."

"Too good. You couldn't stay out of hot water."

"For Christ's sake, none of it was my fault."

And none of it was. During that crazy week in July I had taken on what looked to be three simple cases; and all three had turned into bizarre felonies—two murders involving the theft of a large sum of money and an extortion plot, and the robbery of a diamond ring. One of my clients, the lunatic wife of the first homicide victim, had publicly accused me of criminal negligence and threatened a lawsuit; that had only made things worse. The media had had a field day. First I was a possibly shady character, and then I was a kind of Typhoid Mary who left a wake of disaster everywhere I went, and then, after I managed to come up with solutions in all three cases, I was a supersleuth, Sam Spade and Sherlock Holmes all wrapped up in one package.

As a result, the chief had claimed I was upstaging the police, interfering with the Department's public image, attracting too much crime and too much publicity; it was a matter of public relations, he'd said. And so he had thrown me to the wolves on the State Board, and the wolves had agreed with his view and gobbled up my license. Never mind my unblemished record as a police officer and private investigator for over thirty years; never mind that I had always worked carefully within the law; never mind that I had to eat and had no other means of support. Indefinite suspension. End of hearing, end of reputation, end of career.

Eberhardt clapped me on the shoulder. "Coals are ready," he said. "Come on, we'll go get the steaks."

"I'm not hungry, Eb."

"Me neither. But we got to eat. Otherwise we'll both get shitfaced and start bawling on each other."

"We could quit drinking instead."

"I don't want to quit drinking. I just want to put some food in my belly along with the rest of the beer I plan to swill down."

"All right. I guess it's a good idea."

We went into the kitchen and Eberhardt took the steaks out of the fridge and put them on a plate. Then he got a couple of potatoes, cut them open, smeared them with butter. He was wrapping them in tinfoil, and I was opening two more beers, when the doorbell rang.

"Now who the hell is that?" he said.

"You could answer it and find out."

"One of the neighbors, probably. I got sympathetic neighbors since Dana walked out. I'll be right back."

"Take your time."

He went through the swing door that led into the living room. I finished opening the beer, drained what was left in my previous can, and tasted the fresh one. At the front of the house I could hear Eb opening the door.

Then I heard him say, loudly and clearly, "What the hell—?"

And then there were two sharp echoing reports—gunshots, they could only have been gunshots.

Sudden fear and confusion jerked me around; I went cold all over. In the other room there was the dull sound of something hitting the floor. I slammed the beer can down on the counter, banged the swing door with my shoulder, and charged through into the living room without thinking what I might be letting myself in for.

It was like running onto a Hollywood sound stage where a scene from a gangster movie was being filmed; all sense of reality vanished instantly. Eberhardt was lying on the floor ten feet from the open front door, there was a bleeding hole in his belly, blood all over him, blood on his head, and framed in the doorway was a man standing in a shooter's crouch with a big revolver extended in both hands; I couldn't see much of his face, because the sun was setting on that side of the house and he was just a looming silhouette backlit by its glare, but I had the impression he was Chinese.

I had just enough time to think: *Oh my God!* before he shot me.

He swung the gun in my direction, I saw him do that and I started to throw myself toward the sofa on my left, and all in the same space of time the bullet jarred into the upper part of my chest and I heard the gun crack and the force of impact knocked me sprawling across the carpet. Momentum skidded me behind the sofa; I was aware of burning sensations along my cheek and forearm where they bit into the rough carpet fibers. There was another shot, the metallic whine of a ricochet, the sound of something shattering. A long way off footsteps began to pound on wood, diminishing, gone.

I flopped over on my side, clawed at the back of the sofa

with one hand and swiped the other across my chest. That hand came away bloody—bright primary red glistening, dripping. But there was no pain; the entire upper half of my body felt numb, as if I had been pumped full of a local anesthetic.

Jesus he shot me I'm shot.

Eberhardt, lying over there . . .

I tried to climb the back of the sofa but my legs wouldn't support my weight, the bones and sinew had all melted, my hand kept slipping off the fabric because of the blood, oh, the blood. I slid down again, still with that sensation of melting, as if all of me was dissolving into a puddle of crimson fluid. Outside, far away, people were yelling. My vision turned cloudy; shadows swirled into the room and swallowed the sunlight. But the air stank of burnt gunpowder and spilled blood—I was sharply aware of that.

I crawled out from behind the sofa, swimming through blood and shadow. People were still yelling outside; more footsteps pounded on the porch. And I kept crawling, kept swimming, dragging myself on forearms and knees. I could see Eberhardt in front of me, his body seemed to be the only thing left now in the room. Blood and shadow, blood and shadow. Hole in his belly, wound on the side of his head: torn flesh, scorched flesh. He wasn't moving. Move, Eb, move! And I kept crawling, and his face was the color of ashes.

God, I thought when I got to him—a clear, cold, savage thought—God, he looks dead.

And then there were hands on me, voices all around me, and I let go of the last threads of perception and melted away into the blood and shadow.

Two

THE FIRST TIME I struggled up into consciousness, the room was empty.

It was a hospital room, not the living room in Eberhardt's house. White, sterile, windows with night on the other side; shadows, but no blood. No pain, either—a kind of tingling numbness all over. I moved my feet, moved my right arm, but I could not move my left arm. Fuzziness in my head, as if it had been stuffed with cotton, and a thought pushed its way through and lay in the cotton like something red and pulsing: They cut off my arm. Moment of panic. I struggled on the bed, struggled for more awareness. Then I saw my left arm lying there on the sheet and the panic went away. I kept trying to move my fingers, only nothing happened; the arm just lay there stiff and lifeless.

Another thought: At least I'm alive.

Another: But what about Eberhardt?

I think I called his name. But I was sliding by then, backward down a long chute, and I couldn't stop myself because my arm was dead, and I yelled without voice until the blackness at the bottom of the chute closed over me.

When I came out of it the second time, there was a nurse in a starched white uniform leaning over the bed. She was fat and homely and had a mouth as wide as a child's red sand bucket; she looked a little like Bella Abzug. There was daylight beyond the windows now—cold, gray. I remembered my left arm and tried to move the fingers again. They twitched, spasming, but I could not raise them off the sheet. For the first time I was aware of a dull pain in my left shoulder, in the upper arm all the way to the elbow.

"Don't try to move," the nurse said. "Just lie still."

"Where am I?" It came out in a croak, like somebody trying to imitate a frog—somebody else, not my voice at all.

"San Francisco General."

"My arm . . . I can't move it. . . ."

"Don't try. You're going to be fine."

"Eberhardt," I said. "Is he alive?"

"I'll get Doctor Abrams," she said.

She went out and I lay there trying to think. My mind wouldn't work right; thoughts kept bumping into each other, veering off, breaking up into fragments. Metallic taste in my mouth, but I could not seem to bring up any saliva to wash it away. In my shoulder and arm, the pain thudded arhythmically in cadence with the beat of my heart.

Bella Abzug came back with a thin, cadaverous-looking doctor. He walked over and peeled back one of my eyelids and shone a pencil flashlight into the eye; then he did the same thing with the other eye. He did not have much hair and his forehead and the front part of his scalp were a mass of wrinkles, as if he had too much skin and somebody had grabbed a handful of it and bunched it up on his head. It made him look like a scrawny hound.

He said, "How are your faculties? Can you think clearly, remember what happened to you?"

"Yes."

"Good. We've had you pretty heavily sedated."

"Eberhardt," I said, as I had to the nurse. "Is he alive?"

"Yes. But his condition is critical."

"How critical?"

"He's in a coma," Abrams said.

"Jesus. Will he make it?"

"I can't answer that. He was shot once in the stomach and once under the right ear. It's still touch and go."

"The head wound—how serious is that?"

"Head wounds are always serious."

"Brain damage?"

"Evidently not. But we can't be certain yet."

"What about the stomach wound?"

"Severe internal damage; the bullet struck the sternum and fragmented." He pursed his lips. "We're doing all we can," he said.

"The man who shot us," I said. "Did the police get him?"

"No, not yet. I'll let them talk to you, if you feel up to it."

"Any time."

Abrams nodded. "You don't seem very concerned about yourself," he said then.

"I'm concerned. But the nurse said I'll be all right."

"You will be. The bullet penetrated the fleshy part of your shoulder and lodged near the scapula. We had no real problem in removing it."

"I can't move my arm or my fingers," I said.

"Traumatic neuritis," he said. "Which means there was some damage to the motor nerve, resulting in partial paralysis."

"Temporary or permanent?"

"Temporary. You should regain full use of the arm in time." He paused. "It is possible, though, that there'll be some chronic stiffness, particularly in the thumb and the first three fingers. But I wouldn't worry about it."

No, I thought, it's not your arm. I said, "How long will I be in here?"

"That depends. Another four or five days, I should think."

"What day is it? Monday?"

"Yes. Monday morning."

"Will you let me know as soon as there's any change in Lieutenant Eberhardt's condition?"

"Of course," Abrams said. "I'll send the police in now; they're anxious to talk to you."

I wish I had something to tell them, I thought. But I didn't say that, either.

He took Bella Abzug away with him. I moved my head and looked out through the window at the cold gray light, at the red brick of another hospital wing across the way. Eberhardt. Head shot, gut shot, severe internal damage, lying in a coma somewhere nearby. Doorbell rings on a Sunday afternoon, he goes and opens up, and somebody puts two bullets in him and one in me. Why? For God's sake, *why?*

The door opened again. I swiveled my head on the pillow and watched two men come into the room: Greg Marcus and Ben Klein. Marcus was a lieutenant attached to Homicide, just as Eberhardt was; I knew him slightly. Klein was an old-timer on the force, a sergeant now, a foot-slogger back in the days when I was working at the old Hall of Justice on Kearney and Washington. Like me, he was a good friend of Eb's.

They took the two metal chairs in the room, pulled them up on the left side of the bed. Both of them wore grim expressions and had red-rimmed eyes; they looked as though they had been up all night, and they probably had. When a police officer gets shot, nobody in the investigative end of the Department gets much sleep.

Klein said, the way people always do in these situations, "How do you feel?"

"Shitty."

"Yeah. But the doc says you'll be okay."

I didn't say anything.

Marcus asked, "He fill you in on Eberhardt's condition?"

"Yes."

"Hell of a goddamn thing," Klein said bitterly. He ran a heavy hand across his bulldog jowls, brought it down and made a fist out of it. "It makes you want to hit something. Or somebody."

"You didn't get the guy who did it?"

"Not yet. But we will. Count on it."

"We thought maybe you could give us a description," Marcus said. "You're the only one besides Eberhardt who saw the gunman close up."

"I didn't get much of a look at him," I said. "He was in the doorway when I ran in, but he was backlit by the sun. I think he was Chinese."

"That tallies with what the other witnesses told us. Three neighbors heard the shots, came out in time to see a male Chinese running down the street. They yelled at him but he didn't stop or look around; they couldn't give us much of a description. Short, slender, long hair—that's about all."

Klein said, "Bastard had a car down the block. Neighbors didn't get the license number. They couldn't even tell us the make or model."

Marcus shifted his big athletic body in the chair. "You said you ran in. So you weren't in the living room when Eberhardt was shot?"

"No. I was in the kitchen."

"Doing what?"

"Opening a beer. Eb was getting ready to put a couple of steaks on the barbecue when the doorbell rang."

"Did he say if he was expecting anyone?"

"I don't think he was. He said it was probably one of his neighbors."

"What happened after he left the kitchen?"

"I heard him open the front door. Then he said, 'What the hell?' and there were two shots. Loud. Big gun, wasn't it?"

[15]

"Three-five-seven Magnum," Klein said. "Christ, it's a miracle Eb's still alive. Two Magnum slugs at close range can tear a man apart."

Marcus asked, "How long was it after you heard the shots that you ran into the living room?"

"Couple of seconds. No more."

"And the gunman was in the doorway?"

"Yes. As soon as he saw me, he swung the gun and squeezed off; I didn't have time to get out of the way. Bullet knocked me down back of the sofa. He fired a second round but it was wild."

"Did he say anything at any time?"

"No."

"How old would you say he was?"

"I'm not sure. Young, maybe. It all happened so damned fast."

"Just doesn't add up," Klein said. "The Chinese don't go around shooting white cops, not in this city. They're a close-knit bunch. They blow away their own people often enough—kid-gang rumbles, tong vendettas, all that—but they leave the white community alone. That's the way it's always been."

"Was Eb working on anything in Chinatown?"

"That's the first thing we thought of," Marcus said. "He had a case two weeks ago—Chinese woman fell or was pushed off a fifth-floor walkway in one of the projects. It's still in the open file, but he hadn't been active on it. If there's a connection, we can't figure it. Routine homicide investigation, no apparent drug or underworld ties, no suspects. We're still checking, though."

"What about a revenge motive? Something in Eb's past, somebody he sent up at one time?"

"Negative. The only Chinese he helped put away are either dead or still in prison."

"Friends of theirs? Relatives?"

Marcus shook his blond head. "The most recent case was

six years ago. Friends and relatives don't wait six years to take revenge. Besides, like Ben says, the Chinese just don't handle things that way."

"Hired hand, then?"

"That's possible. There are probably dozens of people in Chinatown who'd wash a body for a price. But it still doesn't add up. Why would a Chinese put out a contract on Eberhardt?"

"Maybe it was a Caucasian who put out the contract."

"Then why use a Chinese gunman? There's plenty of white talent around. And there isn't that much of an inter-racial mix in the underworld; anybody with a grudge against a cop would either do the job himself or hire one of his own kind."

Klein asked me, "Eb ever mention any Chinese names to you?"

"Not that I remember."

"Then he didn't have any Oriental friends?"

"If he did, he never talked about them."

"Not to me, either. Pretty much of a long-shot angle anyway."

"I can think of another long-shot angle," I said.

"Which is?"

"The breakup of Eb's marriage. He didn't know who Dana was involved with, or said he didn't. But maybe there's some sort of connection there."

"I doubt it," Marcus said. "We talked to his wife last night; she showed up here at the hospital as soon as she heard about the shooting. She's living with a man named Samuels down in Palo Alto—law professor at Stanford. We talked to him too. Neither of them has any relationship with a Chinese. And as far as she knows, neither did Eberhardt."

My mouth and throat were dry; I still could not seem to work up any saliva. There was a pitcher of water on the nightstand, and I asked Klein to pour some into a glass for me. He got up and did that.

When I was done drinking, Marcus said, "Let's try another tack. How did Eberhardt seem to you yesterday? Did he act worried, upset?"

"A little. He was still brooding about his marriage breakup."

"Anything else?"

"He said he had some other things on his mind, but he wouldn't talk about them."

"Personal or professional?"

"Might be professional. He said something about hating his job sometimes."

"Did he seem as though he might be expecting trouble?"

"I didn't get that impression, no," I said. "He was just broody."

"He'd been drinking quite a bit, though, hadn't he? Doctor Abrams told us there was a good percentage of alcohol in his blood."

"Just beer, as far as I know. We'd both had seven or eight cans. He might have had a few before I got there, but he wasn't drunk."

The door opened and Abrams put in another appearance. "I'm afraid that's all the time I can allow you, gentlemen," he said to Marcus and Klein.

Marcus said, "We're finished for now," and they both got up. Then he said to me, "I don't think you were a target; the gunman was after Eberhardt and you happened to get in the way. But we've posted an officer outside, just in case."

"Whatever you think best. Will you let me know as soon as anything turns up?"

"For sure."

When the two of them were gone I asked Abrams, "Anybody else waiting to see me?"

"No. There was a woman earlier, but I told her you wouldn't be permitted regular visitors until later today. She said she would be back."

"Was her name Kerry Wade?"

"Yes, it was."

"I want to see her when she comes again," I said.

"If you're awake and feeling up to it. I'm going to give you some more antibiotics; they should make you sleep again for a while."

He rang for Bella Abzug, and she came in and administered the antibiotics. Then she drew the shade over the window and they left me alone in the semidarkness, feeling drowsy and sick and badly used.

But underneath it all was a cold hard knot of anger. Things had seemed pretty grim for Eberhardt and me yesterday; he'd lost his wife and I'd lost Kerry and my license and my livelihood. But now we were both in hospital beds, Eb in a coma fighting for his life, me helpless and weak as a kitten. And somewhere out there was a cold-blooded son of a bitch with a .357 Magnum. It was a lousy goddamned world, full of injustice and full of evil, and there was nothing I could do about it. All I could do was lie here bloated with drugs and bitterness and a growing polyp of hate. That was why I was angry. And I was going to keep on being angry; it was not the kind of rage that goes away easily, or that modulates into self-pity. I was all through with self-pity, with the kind of aimless resignation that had gripped me the past few weeks. Three bullets, two in Eberhardt and one in me, had done more than land the two of us in the hospital, done more than rip open flesh; they had ripped open something else inside me, too, and left a different kind of festering wound.

Those were the last things I thought before the drugs pushed me down into a heavy, dream-haunted sleep. And they were the first things I thought when I woke up again at three o'clock, dehydrated, with hunger pangs and the pain pulsing away in my shoulder.

Angry, damn it. *Angry.*

THREE

THEY LET Kerry visit me at five o'clock.

Bella fed me soup and Jell-o first and then changed the dressing on my shoulder. I saw the wound; it was ugly and bluish, and they had painted it with some sort of dark red antiseptic, and the stitches stood out stark and white. Red, white, and blue. Looking at it made me even more angry. So did the nurse's grave pronouncement that there had been no change in Eberhardt's condition. I was seething inside, but keeping myself tightly wrapped, when Kerry walked into the room.

She came in smiling, but the smile had been pasted on for my benefit; her eyes were solemn and worried, and her face was pale in the auburn frame of her hair. She was wearing an emerald-green dress and a matching coat, as if she had decided bright colors would be more appropriate than mourning gray or black. In one hand she carried a paper sack: present for the patient, a little gesture of her affection for the poor bastard confined to a hospital bed.

The smile faded when she came close enough to take a good look at me. "Hi," she said. "How do you feel?"

"I'm all right."

"Do you . . . does it hurt much? Your shoulder?"

"No."

She stood there looking at me. She had chameleon eyes, the kind that change color with strong rushes of emotion; they were very dark now, an almost black-green.

"God," she said, "I don't know what to say."

"Don't say anything. There's nothing to say."

"I was sick when I heard about it. I came right here to the hospital, but they wouldn't let me see you."

"I know," I said. "I'm glad you came."

She sat down in one of the metal chairs. "I went by your flat this morning," she said. "I still have the key you gave me and I thought you might want a few things. You don't mind, do you?"

"No. What did you bring?"

By way of answering, she opened up the paper sack and let me see what it contained. Some toilet articles and half a dozen pulp magazines. She put it all on the nightstand, folded the sack, and tucked it away in her purse. Then she reached out and touched my right hand, let her fingers rest on it. They were cold and slightly damp, her fingers. I did not move my hand under them.

"I feel terrible about Eberhardt," she said.

"Yeah," I said.

"He's going to die, isn't he."

I gave her a sharp look. "What makes you say that?"

"I heard two of the nurses talking. They said his chances of regaining consciousness were slim."

"He's not going to die."

"Well . . . I hope you're right."

"He's not going to die," I said again.

She was silent for a time. I kept my eyes away from her face because I did not want her to see the anger in them. But she was a perceptive woman; I could feel her watching me.

"You're different," she said after a while.

"My best friend got shot and he's in a coma. I got shot. Yeah, I'm different."

"That's not what I mean. I look at you and I'm not sure I know you anymore. You look the same, but I don't think you are."

"Maybe not," I said.

"Seeing you this way . . . it scares me."

"Why should it scare you?"

"I don't know. But it does."

"Forget it. It's nothing for you to worry about."

"Yes, it is. I care for you, you know that."

"Sure."

"Don't you believe me?"

"I believe you."

She took her hand away from mine, brushed the back of it across my cheek. When I looked at her I saw that there were tears in her eyes.

"It's so damned unfair," she said. "What's happened these past few weeks, what people have done to you. What *I've* done to you."

Same words I had said to Eberhardt on Sunday. But they did not seem to mean much anymore; they were just words. I stared up at the flourescent ceiling lights, not saying anything.

"I'm sorry," Kerry said. "I really am."

"All right."

"I'll make it up to you. Will you let me do that?"

"How?"

"By being with you. By not running away from you anymore."

"I don't want your pity," I said.

"I don't pity you. That's not it."

"You don't love me either. Do you?"

"I don't know. Maybe I can."

"And maybe you can't."

"Don't you want me to try?"

"I'm not sure what I want right now. Except to see the bastard who shot Eb and me behind bars."

"There's nothing you can do about that."

"No," I said, "I guess there isn't."

More silence. She got a handkerchief out of her purse

and wiped her eyes and blew her nose. Then she said, "Do you want me to go?"

"No."

"But you don't seem to want to talk. . . ."

"Not right now. Just sit here with me for a while."

"Yes. All right."

So she sat there and we looked at each other from time to time and the silence grew heavy, a little awkward. I tried to dredge up some of the old feelings for her—the tenderness, the warmth, the love. They were still there but they would not come to the surface; anger and bitterness sealed them off like an iron door. I needed her, I wanted to believe what she'd said to me, and yet the needing was not central. Too many things had happened. Too many things.

At least ten minutes passed without either of us saying a word. Finally she got up and leaned over and kissed me gently on the mouth; her lips, like her fingers, were damp and cold. "I think I'd better leave now," she said.

"Will you come back tomorrow?"

"If you want me to."

"Yes," I said, "I want you to."

"Can I bring you anything else?"

"There's nothing else I need."

She tried the smile again; it was a little wobbly but it stayed in place. "It'll be all right," she said. "You'll see."

"What will?"

"Everything. You, me—Eberhardt."

"Sure."

She seemed to want to kiss me again, but she didn't do it. She said, "I'll see you tomorrow, then," and gathered up her purse and went to the door. I got one more look from there, the poignant kind. Then she was gone.

I spent some more time staring up at the ceiling, not thinking about much. But my mind wasn't blank; I kept getting little blips of memory, scenes from Eberhardt's living room yesterday. Eb lying bloody and twisted on the floor. The Chinese gunman backlit by the sun. The glistening red smears on my hand when I swiped it across my chest. The way the shadows came into the room and swallowed the sunlight. I felt a sudden pain in my right palm, and when I turned the hand over and looked at it I saw little gouged half-moons where I had dug my nails into the skin.

Pretty soon a nurse came in—not Bella Abzug; a black woman, younger and much more attractive—and announced that I had another visitor. I asked her who it was and she said, "Mrs. Dana Eberhardt. Will you see her?"

"Yes. Send her in."

Dana entered the room a couple of minutes after the nurse went away. She was three years younger than Eb and me, just turned fifty, but she didn't look her age; she looked no older than forty. Still slender, except for heavy breasts and wide hips. New hairdo: cut short and curled. There had been gray in the brown hair the last time I'd seen her; she had dyed it away. She looked sleek and fit, despite the gravity of her expression and the dark smudges under her eyes. Life in Palo Alto with a Stanford law professor must be agreeing with her.

"Hello, mug," she said.

Mug. Her pet name for me in the days when she had tried to play matchmaker and marry me off to a variety of eligible women. "You're a mug," she used to say. "You don't know what's good for you. Marriage is a wonderful thing." And now she was living with a law professor, and Eberhardt was lying in a coma with his insides and maybe his head scrambled by a pair of bullets.

I think I hated her a little in that moment.

She came over and stood near the foot of the bed, as if she were afraid to move any closer. "I wasn't sure you'd want to see me," she said.

"It's always nice to see old friends."

I made no effort to keep the bitterness out of my voice,

but she took it without flinching. One of her characteristic gestures was to pick at her chin with thumb and forefinger; she did that. Then she made a throat-clearing sound and wet her lips. They were painted a glossy rust-red color, like drying blood. I had never seen her wear that shade of lipstick before.

"Don't condemn me," she said.

"Why should I condemn you?"

"I still care for Eb. I never wanted to hurt him."

"Then why did you?"

"I couldn't live my life for him any longer. I needed a change, a new direction; I needed to be me."

"So now you are."

"Yes. I've been happy these past few months, mug—"

"Don't call me mug."

"All right. I didn't think you minded the name."

"Well, I do mind it."

"All right."

"Listen, Dana, why're you here? What do you want from me?"

"I don't want anything from you," she said. She sounded hurt. "I just wanted to see you—"

"Give me a little sympathy, is that it?"

"Yes."

"Or maybe you're looking for forgiveness, somebody to tell you you're not a bad woman and none of this is your fault. Well, I'm not that person. Try a rabbi, if that's what you're after."

This time it got to her and she winced. "That's not fair," she said.

"No? Is it fair what happened to Eb?"

She half-turned away from me. But her eyes were clear; she never cried. Maybe that was a significant thing about her, maybe that explained a lot: she never cried.

"Don't you think I feel badly enough as it is?" she said.

"I don't know how you feel. Neither does Eb."

"He must have said terrible things about me. That's why you're acting this way."

"He never said much of anything about you. Except that he thought you were a whore."

"I'm not a whore."

"Maybe not. But you still walked out on him for somebody else."

"It was over between us. He knew that as well as I did."

"The hell he did. You blew him right out of the water, Dana. You tore him up inside."

She put her eyes on me again and I watched anger flash in them. "You weren't married to him. You don't know how he could be."

"I've known him as long as you have."

"But you didn't live with him. You think it's easy, being a cop's wife? Waiting for something like this to happen, some crazy with a gun to show up on your doorstep?"

"You put up with it for twenty-eight years."

"Yes," Dana said, "and I got tired of putting up with it. I got tired of his long hours and his moods and his silences. We never talked anymore. We never went anywhere. We weren't *going* anywhere, can't you understand that? It was over. It had been for a long time."

The rage was thick and hot inside me, tightening my muscles, making the wound in my shoulder throb painfully. But it was not really directed at Dana; she was just a handy object. It was blind, all-encompassing. I was angry at everybody and everything and I wanted to lash out, to hurt someone else.

"Leave me alone, will you," I said. "Go carry on your deathwatch somewhere else. Go back to your goddamn law professor, let him tell you what a poor, misunderstood woman you are."

She pinched her chin again with tremulous fingers. "Damn you," she said. "I came in here feeling sorry for you. I thought we were still friends; I thought you'd understand; I thought we could give each other some comfort. But I was wrong. God, how wrong I was."

"You've been wrong before," I said. "You were wrong three months ago when you moved out of Eb's life."

She pivoted from the bed and went to the door in hard, thumping steps. With the knob in her hand, she looked back at me. "I don't care what you think," she said. "David is a good man, a kind man, and I love him and he loves me. I'm not ashamed of what I did."

"David can go to hell," I said. "So can you."

That stung her too; I saw the pain register in her face before she twisted her head around. She pulled the door open, went through it. When she shut it behind her there was a click like the hammer of a gun being cocked.

It took me a while to calm down, to get myself tightly wrapped again. Then I thought: You were too hard on her, she's suffering too. But I could not seem to feel sorry for her. Eberhardt, yes, but I had no compassion left for anyone else. Least of all myself.

My back hurt from lying in one position; I shifted around on the bed until I was resting on my right hip. But the movement aggravated the pain in my shoulder. A yell formed in my throat and I had to clamp my teeth together to keep it from coming out.

There was one of those hospital buzzers attached to the top of the bed. I grabbed hold of it and jabbed my thumb down on the button. Two minutes later, the young black nurse poked her head inside the door.

"I could use some coffee," I said.

"No coffee. I can bring you some tea."

"Okay. Some tea, then." She started to withdraw, but I stopped her by asking, "Is there any change in Lieutenant Eberhardt's condition?"

"No, I'm afraid not."

"He won't die," I said. "He'll pull through."

She just looked at me.

"He'll pull through, you hear?"

"I'll bring your tea," she said, and when she closed the door it made the clicking sound again—the sound of a .357 Magnum being cocked.

FOUR

TUESDAY.
Greg Marcus came to see me in the morning, alone this time. He still looked haggard and he hadn't bothered to shave the blond stubble off his cheeks. But he had no news, no fresh leads; he only wanted me to go over things again, on the chance that I had forgotten or overlooked something. Grabbing at straws. The police were dead-ended and he knew I knew it. He did not even try to pretend otherwise.

A couple of reporters tried to get in to see me, but I told Abrams and the nurses that I didn't want to talk to them.

Kerry came again in the afternoon. There was less strain between us this time, mainly because she did not try to cheer me up. She just sat and held my hand and endured the protracted silences between the words we said to each other. I was glad when she was there—she was the only person I wanted to see, except for Marcus or Klein with some word on the gunman—but I was just as glad when she was gone and I was alone again.

The nurses fed me three meals and let me get up twice to use the toilet. The rest of the time I slept or stared at the walls. I didn't even make an effort to read the pulp magazines Kerry had brought; I had no interest in reading, no interest in fictional crime or fictional detectives.

Eberhardt was still in a coma, still in critical condition.

And I was still angry.

Wednesday.

I asked for the *Chronicle* and *Examiner* for the past three days and read all the news stories on the shooting and the police investigation. No facts that I didn't already know. But a lot of crap about my background, the loss of my license; I was hot news again and the journalists were making the most of it. I threw the papers on the floor when I was done with them.

Two visitors showed up. One was Litchak, the retired fire inspector who lived in the flat below mine in Pacific Heights. The other was Kerry. I couldn't seem to find much to say to either of them and they didn't stay long.

No change in Eberhardt's condition. Or in mine.

Thursday.

They let me get up and stay up for a while, with my left arm in a sling. As long as I didn't make any sudden moves, I felt almost no pain in my shoulder. But the arm was still stiff; I kept having to make an effort to straighten out all but the little finger on that hand.

Kerry didn't come. She called the head nurse, who passed along a message that she had business obligations at her ad agency and she would come again tomorrow. It mattered that she couldn't make it, and yet it did not matter. I was better off by myself.

Two other guys I knew came to see me. One of them worked on the *Examiner* and the main reason he paid his visit was to get himself an exclusive interview; I threw him out verbally after five minutes.

Eberhardt remained the same. And the police remained stymied: the gunman was still unidentified and still at large.

Friday.

Abrams removed half the stitches and allowed as how the wound seemed to be healing satisfactorily. I asked him when I could get out of there. Tomorrow morning, he said.

Kerry came in the afternoon, very chipper, and made a conspiratorial thing out of giving me a pastrami sandwich she had hidden away in her purse. It was a nice gesture. I told her I was starved for some real food and would wolf the sandwich down after she left, but that was a lie; I had no appetite. I said I would be going home tomorrow, and she said she would drive me and offered to stop by my flat again to pick up some clothes.

Everything else was status quo.

Saturday.

Ben Klein showed up at ten o'clock. Nothing to report. The investigation was not going well, he admitted; nobody in Chinatown was talking, R&I hadn't turned up any possibles on their computer checks, there weren't any leads in Eberhardt's case file or past history or personal effects. He offered to keep a police guard on me for a few more days, but I told him I didn't want that.

After Klein left, Abrams came around with a bunch of instructions on how to care for myself, what I should and shouldn't do, when to come back to have the rest of the stitches taken out. He also gave me some Empirin-and-codeine pills to take if I was bothered by pain.

At eleven-thirty, Kerry arrived with my clothes. I had some trouble getting into the shirt; she had to help me, and afterward she tied on the sling.

And at twelve-fifteen I walked out of the hospital with Kerry hanging on to my good arm. We left through the emergency entrance to avoid any reporters who might be lurking around out front. It was a gray day, foggy and cold, and that was good. I was gray inside, shading toward black;

sunshine would only have fueled my anger by reminding me of the Chinese gunman backlit and half-invisible in the doorway of Eberhardt's house.

Kerry kept up a running stream of chatter on the way crosstown. She had had one of her friends pick up my car, she said, and take it up near my flat; she told me where it was parked. I didn't pay much attention to the rest of what she said.

She had also cleaned up the flat. The dustballs and dirty dishes were gone; the furniture gleamed with polish; the place smelled of lemon-scented air freshener. It didn't look or feel right and it annoyed me. It was like walking into another hospital room—too neat, too antiseptic.

I said, "Why did you clean the place?"

"Well, it was pretty messy. . . ."

"I like it messy. It makes me feel at home."

"I'm sorry. I thought you'd be pleased."

She sounded uncertain and a little hurt. I did not want to be angry at her, of all people; I tightened the wraps on myself and managed a small smile. "It's all right. I'm glad you were concerned."

She came over to kiss me on the cheek. "Are you hungry? I can make something. . . ."

"No. I don't want any food."

"Some coffee?"

"Okay. Some coffee."

She went out into the kitchen. I crossed to the pseudo-Hepplewhite secretary that serves as my desk, rummaged around in one of the drawers with my good hand, and came up with the envelope of old photographs. Eberhardt and me on a fishing trip at Black Point. Eberhardt and Dana in his backyard, with their arms around each other, grinning at the camera. Eberhardt, looking awkward and festive, trimming a tree in his living room one Christmas. A tightness formed in my chest; I put the photographs back into the envelope and the envelope away in the drawer. Taking them out had been a morbid thing to do. I was not even sure why I had done it.

Kerry came in with the coffee and we sat on the couch and looked at each other. She said, "Do you want to talk?"

"About what?"

"About what's bothering you."

"You know what's bothering me."

"Yes, but it's doing things to you I don't understand."

"I don't understand them myself," I said.

"So you don't want to talk?"

"No. Not now."

"It's just that I feel—"

"What?"

"That you're shutting me out. Shutting everybody out, withdrawing into yourself. It scares me."

"You said that on Monday."

"I can't help it. I've felt that way all week."

"Don't worry about me," I said.

"But I do."

"I'll be fine. When Eberhardt wakes up, when the bastard who shot us is locked away . . . then I'll be just dandy."

"What if either or both of those things don't happen?"

"They'll happen."

"But what if they don't?"

"They'll happen," I said again. "Let's drop the subject, okay? I'm not in any mood for it."

We were quiet for a time. Then she said, "Do you want me to stay here with you?"

"For a while, yes."

"I meant tonight. For a few days."

"I wouldn't be much good to you with this arm."

"I wasn't talking about sex. Is that what you thought?"

"I didn't think anything."

"What kind of person would I be if that's all I had to offer you?"

"All right. Let it go."

"I don't think you should be alone," she said.

"No? Why not?"

"Because you'll brood. I know you that well; when you're alone and upset, you brood."

"I won't brood."

"Then you don't want me to stay?"

"No. I need to be alone."

"Just tonight? Or don't you want to see me at all?"

"I didn't say that. *You* said that six weeks ago, remember?"

"Yes," she said in a small voice, "I remember."

I felt bad for her again. "Kerry, look, I'm not shutting you out. I'm glad you care for me, I'm glad you want to be with me; maybe there's still something for us after all. But too much has happened to me, too fast. I've got to come to terms with it and I've got to do it my own way. You've already given me what I need from you—being there, caring. Keep on being there, okay?"

"I will," she said, and for a moment I thought she was going to cry. But it didn't happen. Her face smoothed and she put on a smile. Then she took my good hand, held it in both of hers; her fingers were very strong and very cold.

We did not say much to each other after that, but it was a good kind of silence. She left at four, saying she would call tomorrow, come by if I wanted her to. When she was gone I felt relieved and sorry at the same time, the way I had each time she'd left my room at the hospital.

I sat and stared at the walls. Made myself some more coffee. Stared at the walls again until the room itself began to bother me. It was just too neat, too clean; I hated it this way, it wasn't mine any longer. I got up and went into the bedroom and took some clothes out of the dresser and scattered them around in there and in the living room. I took a handful of pulps off the shelves that flanked the bay window, scattered those around. I found some mildewed cheese in the refrigerator, put it on a plate and put the plate on the coffee table next to the dirty cups. I was breathing heavily when I was finished. The place looked better then, it looked all right. Familiar. Mine again.

The phone rang at seven o'clock. Newspaper reporter, wanting an interview; I banged the receiver down in the middle of his pitch, so hard I almost knocked the thing off the nightstand.

The anger was still there an hour later, when I struggled out of my clothes and got into bed. It was always there now; it had not left me for a minute since Monday. Living and growing in my body, sometimes burning hot and sometimes banked, clinging to me and making me cling to it— a symbiotic thing that was both friend and enemy.

Sunday.

I was awake before dawn, with pain pulsing in my shoulder because I had shifted somehow in my sleep and wrenched the arm. I got up and took one of the pills Abrams had given me. In the bathroom I looked at myself in the medicine cabinet mirror. Beard stubble, but not enough to make me want to shave again; I had shaved yesterday before leaving the hospital. My eyes looked dark, sunken. But the anger was not visible in them, at least not to me. Windows with the blinds drawn tight behind them.

When the pain diminished I took my left arm out of the sling and spent several minutes trying to flex it. I could not quite get it straightened out all the way; the pain came back, sharp stabs of it, whenever I tried to lock the elbow. The fingers moved all right, unbent into horizontal planes, but when I went to pick up a glass I couldn't close them around it.

The whole time I kept thinking about Eberhardt. He had been in a coma one week, seven days, 160 hours. How long could he hang on that way, balanced on the thin edge between life and death? Weeks, months? Years? I had heard of cases where people lay in a coma for two, three, four years, little more than vegetables kept breathing by life-support equipment. If that happened to Eberhardt . . .

Restlessly, I went back into the bedroom and called the Hall of Justice. Neither Marcus nor Klein was in, and nobody else would tell me anything, even when I explained who I was. I ended the call by jamming down the handset. Damn the cops; I was beginning to hate the Department. A few individuals like Klein and Marcus were all right, but it was not being run the way it had been in the old days. The damn brass all seemed to have political ties and ambitions; they went around yelling about public relations, the police image, the war on crime. And yet they were also close-mouthed, secretive, unyielding, like a bunch of neo-fascists. The chief had yanked my license because I was too good a cop myself, because I made waves and showed them up and undercut their authority. A victim of a goddamn fascist purge, that was what I was when you boiled it down.

Out in the kitchen I banged some pots and pans around, making coffee and frying a couple of eggs for breakfast. It was awkward trying to cook with one hand; I spilled coffee on the counter, broke both egg yolks, spattered hot butter on myself. By the time I scooped the eggs out onto a plate, I was growling again and spewing blasphemy all over the kitchen.

The telephone rang. I went and hauled up the receiver and barked a hello. A whiny male voice said my name questioningly, and as soon as I heard it my hand went tight around the receiver.

It was an Oriental voice—Chinese.

I said, "Yes. What is it?"

"I having something to tell you. About shooting, you and Lieutenant Eb-hardt."

I eased down on the bed. "Who is this?"

"No. Not giving my name."

"What do you want to tell me?"

"Man who do shooting—Mau Yee."

"Mau Yee? That's his name?"

"No. *Mau Yee.*"

"I don't understand. . . ."

"You finding out. Mau Yee. That's all."

I thought he was going to hang up. "Wait a minute! Why call me about this? Why didn't you call the police?"

"No police," he said.

"Why not? If you have information . . ."

"No police. You lieutenant's friend, you getting shot too. Maybe you understand."

"Understand what?"

"Reason for shooting."

"No. Why did this Mau Yee shoot Eberhardt?"

"You not knowing?"

"I'm asking you, man. Why?"

Hesitation. And then he said, "Bribe. Big bribe."

"What!"

"Yes. Big bribe. You understand now?"

"Hell, no, I don't understand. Are you trying to tell me Eberhardt was taking bribes from somebody in Chinatown?"

"Not in Chinatown. Somebody else."

"That's a frigging lie!"

"No lie. You see why I not calling police? You lieutenant's friend, you find out."

"Goddamn it, who are you? What do you know? Talk to me!"

The line clicked and went dead.

I sat holding the receiver, shaking a little. Then I cradled it, carefully, to keep the impulse for violence bottled up, and went out into the living room and took a couple of hard turns around it.

No, I thought, not Eberhardt. Dirty? Him? No. He was an honest cop; I'd known him for thirty years, I'd worked with him, I'd listened to the hatred in his voice when he talked about police officers on the take. He wasn't dirty, he couldn't be.

Crank call, I thought. But it hadn't sounded like a crank call. And Chinese weren't prone to that kind of thing; of all the cranks who annoyed police and other people, almost none of them were Orientals.

Mau Yee, I thought. Who the hell is Mau Yee?

And who the hell is the man on the phone?

Big bribe. Not in Chinatown. Somebody else.

It just wasn't possible that Eberhardt was taking. And yet he'd been shot by a Chinese gunman, and the caller had been Chinese, and Mau Yee was a Chinese name or phrase. All of that fit together; why would the man have lied about the other thing?

You see why I not calling police? You lieutenant's friend, you find out.

I stopped pacing. Without even thinking about it, I crossed to the closet and got my overcoat out and shrugged it over my shoulders. When I had it buttoned I hunted around until I found where Kerry had put my car keys, on top of the mantelpiece.

Yeah, I thought then, grimly. I'll find out, all right.

I'll find out.

FIVE

OUTSIDE IT WAS COLD and foggy again, the kind of heavy dripping fog that tends to linger for days during the summer months. I was shivering when I got to where my car was parked a block from the flat. Doctor Abrams had told me to stay inside, get plenty of rest, don't exert myself. The hell with him. The hell with everybody. It was my life and I could do what I damned well pleased with it. I didn't have a license anymore, I only had one good arm, but I still had the freedom of choice; they hadn't taken that away from me yet.

I started the car, put the heater on high, and sat there until some of the chill went away. Driving with one hand was no real problem because the car had an automatic transmission; I wheeled it around and took it to Van Ness. Twenty minutes later I rolled down the steep Castro Street hill into Noe Valley.

There was not much activity on Eberhardt's block of Elizabeth Street. No kids playing; nobody out puttering in his garden or mowing his lawn or washing his car; nobody drinking beer and cooking steaks on the backyard barbecue. The absence of sunshine kept everyone indoors or off on day trips somewhere. The weather made a big difference in people's lives in this city. So could a few weeks, and one week in particular. Seven days could make all the difference in the world—turn you upside down and inside out, reshape your thinking, restructure the patterns of your life.

And maybe force you to accept things you never would have believed and never wanted to know.

The curb in front of Eberhardt's house was empty; I parked there, went up the path, and climbed the stairs onto the porch. The house was locked tight, but there was no problem in that. Eb had given me a key years ago, the way friends do. I found it on my key ring, slid it into the latch, and let myself in.

The living room was dark, full of shadows again. The blood was there too, dried into the carpet where Eberhardt had lain, where I had crawled across it from the sofa. His blood, my blood. I imagined I could smell the burnt gunpowder on the cold musty air. Little shivers crawled up my back; a ghost pain slid along the length of my stiffened left arm. The whole thing from last Sunday replayed itself in my mind in ragged blips, like scenes in a badly cut *film noir*.

Dry-mouthed, I crossed to the staircase and clumped up to the second floor. It was better up there; the images faded, the phantom smell was gone. I bypassed Eb's bedroom and the adjacent guest room and opened the last door on the left. Originally it had been a third bedroom, but he had converted it into an office for himself when he and Dana bought the house.

More shadows; I went over to the window, opened the curtains to let some light in. Desk, sideboard, Naugahyde couch, over-stuffed chair, a small bookcase with some police manuals and a few other books jammed into it in haphazard fashion, a long table supporting a partially finished model railroad layout that he had been fiddling with for years; an electric Olympia beer sign on one wall, on another a framed photograph of our Police Academy graduating class. It was Eberhardt's room in every way, a perfect reflection of the man I had known for three decades. His sanctuary, he'd called it. Nobody touched anything in there but him.

Except that somebody *had* touched things—Marcus or

Klein, probably, looking for a lead to explain the sudden attack. A couple of the desk drawers were half open, papers were spread around on the desktop in a non-Eberhardt way; an accordian file stood open on the sideboard. If there was anything incriminating among his papers, had they found it? Either Marcus or Klein might have told me if they had, but then again they might not have. Cops did not go around spreading the word when one of their number turned up dirty; they would keep it under wraps as long as they could, until a full investigation had been conducted.

Still, they would have made the search early in the week, not later than Monday when no other leads opened up and it became clear that Eberhardt wasn't going to regain consciousness right away, and I had talked to both Klein and Marcus later on. If they had discovered something incriminating, I should have been able to tell it from what they said and the way they acted. Klein especially, because he was almost as close to Eb as I was; he wore his feelings as openly as he'd worn his patrolman's badge.

So the odds were that they had come up empty. But did Klein know about Eb's hideaway safe? I knew about it because he had told me, shown it to me once. He had also given me the combination, for the same reason he had given me the key to the house. In case of an emergency, he'd said. In case anything happened to him.

The safe was built into the bottom of the sideboard, concealed by a horizontal sliding panel. A small thing, just large enough to hold documents and a few valuables. I squatted in front of the sideboard, opened the doors. On top of the panel were some glasses and a bottle of brandy; I took them out, slid the panel aside to expose the combination dial, and opened my address book to the set of numbers I had written down in back. Half a minute later I hauled the safe door up and peered inside.

There was not much to see. A small jewelry case that contained his wedding ring; I remembered that he had stopped wearing it after Dana moved out. An envelope with five twenty-dollar bills in it—but that didn't mean anything. Mad money, probably, or a small cache for emergencies. His marriage license. A packet of U.S. savings bonds that amounted to fifteen hundred dollars. An insurance policy. A savings account passbook that showed a balance of $532.57. And a stock-transfer form, made out in Eberhardt's name, turning over to him one thousand shares of Mid-Pacific Electronics.

I knelt there for a time, staring at the stock-transfer thing. I did not like the look of it; it made my stomach feel hollow and made me afraid. Eberhardt had never dabbled in the stock market, never owned any stocks so far as I knew. He wasn't a gambler and he didn't trust that sort of investment. So what was he doing with a piece of paper like this? It was not a regular transaction, the kind where you go to a broker and buy shares of a common stock. Somebody owned those thousand shares—somebody whose name did not appear on the form, who had neither filled it out completely nor signed it to make the transfer binding. Eb had no close relatives; it couldn't be anything like that. Then who? And why?

Mid-Pacific Electronics. I had never heard of it. There were plenty of electronics firms in Northern California, with the boom in the computer and related industries; it could be a large or a small company, and the value of those thousand shares could also be large or small. If they weren't worth much, maybe Eb *was* taking a flyer—maybe somebody had given him a tip and the owner of the stock was unloading it piecemeal to friends and other investors. He might have changed his mind about gambling in the market. Dana's defection had changed him in a lot of ways; this could be one of them.

Big bribe. Not in Chinatown. Somebody else.

But he could have changed that way, too, I thought bitterly. Honest people do turn crooked; honest cops do start taking bribes. And the bribes they take don't have to be in cash, either, not in this day and age.

I put the form in my coat pocket, returned the rest of the stuff to the safe, closed the lid and spun the dial to lock it, and then slid the panel back into place and rearranged the glasses and the bottle of brandy. When I straightened up I took another look around the room. But there did not seem to be much point in doing any more searching; Eb had no other safes or hiding places that I knew about, and the police would have been through everything else.

Downstairs again, I tried not to look at the bloodstained carpet. No good; it drew my eyes magnetically. They could have cleaned it up, I thought. Or Dana could have come and done that—aired the place out, made it decent for Eb when he came home. It didn't surprise me that she hadn't been here. She wanted no part of this house anymore, no part of Eberhardt's life; she was back in Palo Alto, waiting in her law professor's bed to find out if Eb lived or died.

I hope she's still suffering a little, I thought. I hope she has long nights and bad dreams.

I made a promise to myself that I would come back in a few days and call a cleaning service and have them pick up the carpet. Maybe nobody else cared about those stains, but I did. At least I could see to it that they were erased from the carpet, even if I could never erase them from my memory, or Eberhardt from his.

On the way back to Pacific Heights I made two stops. The first was at a liquor store on 24th Street, where I bought a copy of the *Sunday Examiner–Chronicle.* There was nothing on the front page about Eb or the police investigation. Other news, national and local, had kicked it onto one of the inside pages, or maybe too much time had passed and they had quit writing about it altogether; I didn't bother to look. Instead I turned to the financial section and checked for a stock listing on Mid-Pacific Electronics.

No listing. Which meant what? Either the company was

too small or too insolvent to warrant one, I thought, or else they had not gone public with their stock. In any case, it would take some checking to find out how much a share of Mid-Pacific was worth, and just what kind of outfit it was.

My second stop was at a service station on Market, to get a tankful of gas and to have a look at the directory in their public telephone booth. There was a local listing for Mid-Pacific Electronics, it turned out: an address on Pine Street in the Financial District. I thought about dialing the number, but I didn't do it. Even if anyone was around on Sunday, which was unlikely, I wanted more information before I started asking questions of the company personnel.

All the parking places near my building were taken; I had to leave the car three blocks away and walk uphill. By the time I let myself into my flat, I was winded and coated with an oily sweat. I shrugged out of my overcoat—and the telephone bell went off.

It was Kerry. "My God," she said, "where have you been?"

"Why?"

"I tried to call you a little while ago and there was no answer. You didn't go out, did you?"

"No. I was sleeping."

"Didn't you hear the phone?"

"I turned the bell down on it."

Pause. Then she said, "You sound . . . odd."

"I just woke up. I'm a little groggy."

"Are you all right?"

"Yes."

"How's your arm?"

"Still stiff. No pain, though."

"That's good. Did you eat something?"

"I fried a couple of eggs," I said.

Another pause. "Well, I've been thinking," she said. "How about if I bake a lasagna and bring it over? We could have a quiet dinner together—"

[44]

"No. Not today."

"Why not?"

"I wouldn't be very good company. Maybe tomorrow night."

"Are you *sure* you're all right?"

"I'm fine. Just not in the mood for visitors."

"Well . . . I'll be here if you need me."

"I know you will."

"I'll call you in the morning, if I don't hear from you sooner."

"No, let me call you."

"Why? You're not planning to go out somewhere tomorrow . . ."

"I'll call you," I said and put the receiver down.

My stomach was growling; I hadn't eaten the eggs I'd fried earlier; I hadn't eaten anything all day. I dumped the cold eggs out of the pan, fried some more, and washed them down with gulps of milk. Then I went back to bed. There was nothing I could do until tomorrow; Mid-Pacific Electronics would have to wait until then.

So would Mau Yee, the son of a bitch, whoever and whatever he was.

Six

At nine-thirty Monday morning I was sitting in a cubicle at the Hall of Justice with an inspector named Richard Loo. I did not know him, but he knew who I was; there wasn't a cop in the city who didn't know who I was these days. When I went up to General Works and told the desk man I wanted to see somebody on the Gang Task Force, I had to wait less than five minutes before Loo came out. Two minutes after that we were in the cubicle for a private talk.

The Gang Task Force had been formed in 1977, when a pair of Chinese youth gangs—the foreign-born Wah Ching and the American-born Chung Ching Yee or "Joe Boys," named after its leader—had gone on a rampage against each other over territorial rights to gambling and extortion rackets. There had been open warfare on the streets, several shootings and killings in and out of Chinatown, and it had culminated when three Joe Boys armed with automatic weapons walked into a popular Washington Street restaurant one Sunday night and opened fire on a group of Wah Ching; five people had been killed and eleven others injured. The Golden Dragon Massacre, as the media called it after the name of the restaurant, had made headlines all over the country and led to the mayor posting a $25,000 reward for information leading to the conviction of the gunmen. The Gang Task Force, comprised of white and Oriental cops, had tracked down the perpetrators and put an end to the warfare. In order to keep it from flaring up again, and to maintain a close watch on underworld activities in the Chinese community, they remained an active arm of the Department.

Loo had been with the task force since its inception, he told me. He was in his late thirties, polite, quiet, studious-looking in a pair of wire-rimmed glasses and a neat business suit. He shook my good hand with an air of respectful solemnity, murmured sympathetic words about Eberhardt and what had happened to me; I got the impression that he was apologizing, not for himself but for the Chinese population in general, and that in his own way he was just as angry as I was. On the way to the cubicle he wondered solicitously if I ought to be up and around so soon. I told him I was a fast healer, lied about how I felt, and he let it go at that.

Now, sitting across a table from me, he said, "I'm afraid I don't have much to tell you. All the doors seem to be closed in Chinatown. The shooting of a police officer . . . well, no one wants to get involved."

I was there to ask him about Mau Yee, but I did not want to make him suspicious by doing it straight out. There would be a way to work in the question later on. I said, "What about the case Eberhardt was working on? The death of a woman in one of the projects?"

"Doesn't seem to be anything there. The woman, Polly Soon, fell from a walkway at the Ping Yuen project on Pacific—fifth-floor walkway, right outside her apartment. She was a common hooker, worked the bars along Grant and in North Beach."

"Could she have been murdered?"

"The coroner didn't find anything to make us think so," Loo said. "Neither did the lieutenant. I talked to the same people he did, including an informer named Kam Fong; none of Polly Soon's neighbors saw it happen, no one claims to know anything about it. She didn't work with a pimp; strictly free lance. Half a dozen arrests for soliciting, but that's all—no underworld ties of any kind. I think her death was probably an accident."

"This informer—Kam Fong, did you say?"

"Yes."

"Had Eberhardt used him before?"

"A time or two. Fong is a drug addict, but his information is generally reliable; I use him myself."

I made a mental note of the name. "Could there be a connection between Fong and the shooting?"

"I doubt it. I've known him for years; he's a low-life, but he wouldn't have anything to do with violence against a police officer. I'm as sure of him as one can be of such people."

Loo did not have a very high opinion of drug addicts or informers. Or of anyone, no doubt, who failed to walk the straight and narrow in Chinatown. Chinese cops tended to be less tolerant of the criminal element among their race than any other ethnic group. It had to do with pride; the Chinese were a fiercely proud people.

I asked, "What about paid assassins? There can't be that many in Chinatown who'd take a contract on a cop."

He made a wry mouth. "More than you'd think. *Boo how doy*—body-washers for the criminal tongs, most of them former youth-gang members. I know at least three Hui Sip who might do it for the right price."

"Hui Sip?"

"The tong that controls most of the gambling in Chinatown, among other things. But they're clever; we haven't been able to get enough on the elders to put them away."

"Are there many tongs like that these days?"

"Not many, no," Loo said. "Most of them are fraternal, harmless social clubs. The Six Companies keeps a tight rein on them. But there are still a couple. They're the ones who corrupt the kids, get them to do their dirty work."

The Chinese Six Companies was an organization founded

in the nineteenth century to oversee and mediate activities within the community, and to work for betterment of the lot of Chinese in America. Their authority had been shaken somewhat in recent years, but they were still the ruling force in Chinatown.

I said, "You've talked to some of the body-washers?"

"Yes. With negative results."

"How about one called Mau Yee?"

Loo looked surprised. "You know of Mau Yee?"

"I've heard the name," I said carefully.

"A bad one. Not a cat, that boy—a snake."

"Cat?"

"Mau Yee means 'The Cat.' His street name."

"What's his real name?"

"Jimmy Quon. An ABC—American-born Chinese—and one of the original Joe Boys."

"Young guy, then?"

"Yes. Mid-twenties. He belongs to Hui Sip now; one of the three *boo how doy* I mentioned." Loo shook his head. "A bad one," he said again. "We've linked him to at least three murders in the past six years, but never with enough evidence for an indictment."

"Was he one of those you talked to?"

"One of the first. But he has an alibi for the time of the shooting."

"How strong?"

"We couldn't shake it. He was playing *pai gow* with three other tong members, he claimed, and each of the three backed him up."

I did not want to press for any more information on Jimmy Quon; I had what I'd come for, and I could find Quon all right on my own. I asked Loo a few more general questions, to ease out of the interview, and then thanked him for his time and got on my feet.

He said as we shook hands again, "We may not have uncovered much so far, but it's only a matter of time before we get a break. Sooner or later we'll find out who pulled the trigger."

"Sure," I said. "Sooner or later."

I left him and rode the elevator down to the lobby. There was a bank of telephone booths off to one side; I entered one, opened the telephone directory. No listing for Jimmy Quon. But there was a listing for a Kam Fong, on Jackson Street. I wrote down the address and number in my notebook.

But I was not ready to look him up yet, or to do anything about Jimmy Quon. I needed more information on Mid-Pacific Electronics first, a better handle on that stock-transfer form I'd found in Eberhardt's safe. If there was a connection between Mid-Pacific and the shooting, if Eberhardt *was* dirty, it would make plenty of difference in how I handled things with Mau Yee.

I drove down to the Financial District, put my car in a parking garage on Montgomery, and wandered around until I came to a small brokerage firm called Waller & Company. Inside, I told the receptionist I wanted to talk to someone about a stock purchase, and she set me up with a guy named Leo Vail.

Vail didn't seem to recognize me; the photographs that had appeared in the newspapers had not been particularly good likenesses. Which was fine. I did not want to give him my right name because it would only lead to a bunch of questions. I said I was Andrew James and he bought that all right. He didn't say anything about my arm being in a sling and I didn't offer an explanation.

I said, "I'm interested in making a stock investment. A friend of mine told me about a company called Mid-Pacific Electronics, said they'd be a good buy, but I don't know anything about them. So I thought I'd better check them out."

Vail was in his fifties, gray-haired and energetic. He shifted around in his chair; you could see him thinking, sifting through his memory. "Mid-Pacific Electronics," he said at length. "I've heard the name, but they're not on the Exchange and I'm not familiar with them. If you don't mind waiting a bit, I'll see what we've got in our computer files."

"No problem. Take your time."

He went away somewhere. I sat and listened to people talking on the telephone, the clattering of machines. My left arm felt stiff and sore; I kept trying to flex the fingers, without much success. What if the arm stiffens up for good? I thought. What if I come out of this a cripple?

The hell with it, I thought. Eberhardt could come out with a lot worse than a stiffened arm.

It was ten minutes before Vail came back. He had a computer printout in one hand and he plunked it down on the desk as he sat again. "Sorry I took so long," he said. "Computer was being used."

"That's okay."

"Let's see," he said. He glanced over the printout. "Uh-huh. Yes. Mid-Pacific is a small firm, established in 1977. They haven't gone public yet, but it seems that they're planning to shortly."

"A reputable outfit?"

"Oh yes. Quite respectable. And quite successful, evidently. They manufacture a component for industrial computers. One of the founders, Carl Emerson, owns a patent on it—some sort of revolutionary component, according to our data. That would explain Mid-Pacific's overnight success in the field."

"How many other founders besides Emerson?"

"Two. Philip Bexley and Orin Tedescu."

"Tedescu. Is that T-e-d-e-s-c-u?"

"Yes, that's right."

"Do the three of them own all the company stock?"

"Yes. Emerson appears to have controlling interest, though."

"Why are they planning to go public, do you know?"

"Not specifically, no. But I imagine it's to raise capital for purposes of expansion. That's the usual reason."

"So you think Mid-Pacific would be a good buy?"

"I'd have to do some more investigating before I could recommend it," Vail said. "But on the surface, yes, it would seem to be an excellent buy."

"I don't suppose there's any way of knowing yet what the stock will sell for."

"Not until they announce how large a block they're putting on the market. How many shares would you be interested in?"

"I don't know. Say a thousand."

"Well, if that much is available, and if the company continues to flourish, it could be a very lucrative investment. There are no guarantees, of course, but . . . it does look promising. Would you like me to gather more data for you, Mr. James?"

"If you would, I'd appreciate it."

"Certainly."

"How long will it take?"

"Oh, a day or so. If you'll just give me your address and a number where I can reach you . . ."

"I'm leaving for Los Angeles on business pretty soon," I said, "and I don't plan to be home much in the interim. Could I call you instead?"

"Of course. Tomorrow, around this time?"

"Fine."

He gave me one of his cards and I tucked it away in my wallet. He said it had been a pleasure; I said yes, it had. Then I went back out on the street to hunt up a telephone booth.

Emerson, Bexley, and Tedescu. Three names—three possibles. If they owned all of the Mid-Pacific stock, then it had to be one of them who had given Eberhardt that stock-transfer form. But why? What was the common denominator that linked a police lieutenant, a Chinese body-washer, and an outfit that manufactured a component for computers?

I found a phone booth in the lobby of one of the larger office buildings on Montgomery. Neither Emerson, Bexley, nor Tedescu was listed in the San Francisco directory. Which meant that they each had unlisted numbers, or lived somewhere outside the city, or both. I could go to the Pacific Telephone offices and look through the directories for the nine Bay Area counties, but that would take too much time and might not get me anything. There was a better way to handle it.

I put through a long-distance call to Ben Chadwick in Hollywood, charging it to my home phone. Chadwick was a private investigator who specialized in work for the major film companies, and he had done a favor or two for me in the past. When I got him on the line he spent a couple of minutes talking about the loss of my license and the shooting, what a shame it all was, how sorry he felt. But he sounded sincere. He was a pretty decent guy.

I finally got him off that by saying, "I need a favor, Ben. Nothing major; I'd do it myself if I could, but all my pipelines are closed up these days."

"You're not working, are you? Without a license?"

"No," I lied. "It's a favor for a friend."

"Yeah, sure. What is it you need?"

"A check on three men who live up here—addresses, whether or not they have criminal records, that sort of thing. You've got police and DMV contacts; it shouldn't take long. Can do?"

He sighed. "I suppose so. Who are they?"

"Carl Emerson, Philip Bexley, Orin Tedescu." I spelled Tedescu's name for him. "They own a company called Mid-Pacific Electronics. See if you can find out anything about that, too."

"Okay. You still have your office?"

"Yes, but the phone's disconnected. And I don't know

[53]

when I'll be home. I'll call you back later today."

"I should be here. Take it easy, huh?"

"You know me," I said.

"That's what I mean," he said, and rang off.

When I came out of the building I turned north and walked up to Pine. I wanted a look at the offices of Mid-Pacific Electronics now, and if I could manage it, a look at Emerson and Bexley and Tedescu.

SEVEN

THE BUILDING THAT HOUSED Mid-Pacific Electronics was one of the newer Financial District high-rises—sculptured facade with plenty of glass, marble-floored lobby, brass-trimmed elevators, and a bank on the ground floor to lend it all an air of ultra-respectability. According to the directory, Mid-Pacific had its offices on the fifteenth floor, right near the top. I got into one of the elevators and let it whisk me up in padded silence.

When the thing stopped and the doors whispered open, a beefy guy in a hurry almost ran me down. I managed to avoid him, and he blinked at me and said, "Sorry," as he maneuvered himself into the elevator. He was in his thirties, wearing a three-piece suit, and what hair he had was dust-colored and wispy, like a skullcap made out of lint. He jabbed one of the buttons, giving my arm sling a curious glance. I turned away from him, but there was a full-length mirror on the opposite wall; I had a glimpse of him fiddling with his hand-painted tie before the doors slid shut.

On both sides of the mirror were brass arrows and brass numerals to let you know where the various offices could be found. 1510 was down to the right. The lettering on the door, when I got to it, said *Mid-Pacific Electronics* in fancy scrolled brass. I rotated the knob and went inside.

The anteroom was tastefully decorated, with a couple of chairs, a table that had some magazines on it, and a reception desk behind which were a couple of unmarked doors.

The desk was occupied by an efficient-looking young woman, attractive if you liked females who wore gold-rimmed glasses on a thin gold chain. She was stuffing envelopes with what looked to be invoices, but she quit doing that as I entered. The smile she gave me was professional and did not have much candlepower behind it.

"May I help you?"

"Yes. My name is Andrew James. I'd like to see Mr. Emerson, please."

"I'm afraid he's not in. He'll be at our Peninsula plant all day. Was it a business matter?"

"More or less. How about Mr. Bexley? Is he in?"

"No, you just missed him. He left not more than three minutes ago."

"Big fellow wearing a three-piece suit and a hand-painted tie?"

"Yes, that's right."

"We bumped into each other out at the elevators," I said. "We've never met, though, so I didn't know who he was."

"Yes, sir."

"Well—is Mr. Tedescu available?"

"He's in his office, yes, but he may be busy. May I tell him why you're here?"

"It has to do with your company stock. I understand Mid-Pacific is going public soon and I'm interested in buying shares when that happens."

"I see," she said. "Will you have a seat, please?"

I had a seat. She got up and went through one of the doors, closing it behind her. I looked at the magazines on the table; except for a copy of *Fortune,* they all dealt with the electronics industry and most were trade publications. I didn't open any of them. It would have been like trying to read something written in a foreign language.

The secretary came back pretty soon, leaving the inner

door open this time. "Mr. Tedescu will see you, Mr. James," she said. "Follow me, please."

She led me down a short corridor past two more closed doors into a good-sized office at the far end. The room was cluttered but not messy, dominated by a massive oak desk and a table with draftsman's tools and electronic designs spread over its surface. A short, plump man stood behind the desk, between it and three tall windows. The view in which he was framed would have been impressive on a clear day; now, under the overcast sky, the city and bay beyond looked gray and dismal, as if all the color had been bleached out of them.

The secretary went away and the plump guy came around the desk to greet me. He was in his forties, dark-haired, and the ruptured blood vessels in his cheeks marked him as a habitual drinker. He also had the biggest pair of ears I had ever seen, the kind that would have saddled him with the nickname Dumbo when he was a kid. But he didn't seem self-conscious about the ears; in fact, he wore his dark hair in an old-fashioned brush cut, as if to emphasize their jug-handle quality. A badge of distinction in an otherwise non-descript appearance.

"Mr. James?" he said, giving me his hand. "I'm Orin Tedescu."

"Pleased to meet you, Mr. Tedescu."

"Same here." He had a sharp, penetrating gaze and he used it to size me up as we shook hands. But there was no recognition in it; if he knew or suspected who I was, he managed to conceal the knowledge. "What happened to your arm? An accident?"

"Yes," I said, "an accident."

"Too bad. I broke my leg once a few years ago; fell off a bicycle. Can you imagine that?" He wagged his head in a rueful way. "Well, Miss Addison tells me you're interested in buying some of our stock."

"I may be, yes."

"A wise choice—you won't regret it. Here, have a seat. I can only give you a few minutes, I'm afraid; I'm on a tight schedule today."

"I understand."

I sat in one of two visitors' chairs, and Tedescu went around behind the desk again and plopped himself down in his own chair. It was big and wide, made of leather and oak, and it dwarfed him somewhat. Unlike his partner, Bexley, he didn't look much like a typical business executive. He was wearing casual slacks and a blue shirt open at the throat, and there were bluish stains on his hands—ink of some kind.

He put his elbows on the chair arms, laced his pudgy fingers together. The smile he gave me seemed genuine. "So," he said. "You're a speculator, Mr. James?"

"Not exactly, no."

"What is it you do for a living?"

"I'm a small businessman," I said.

"Electronics-related?"

"No. I own a chain of laundromats. They make me enough so I can afford to dabble in the market."

"Have you been successful at that, too?"

"I've done pretty well. My broker keeps after me to expand my portfolio, but I guess I'm too cautious to tie up all my extra capital."

"May I ask who your broker is?"

"Waller and Company."

He nodded. "A good firm. Are they the ones who told you about Mid-Pacific?"

"Actually, no," I said. "I have a friend in the electronics industry, works for an arm of IBM. He heard you were going public and suggested Mid-Pacific might be a good investment."

"And that's why you're here? Size us up, find out more

about us before you decide to take the plunge?"

"Yes. I'm the cautious type, as I said."

"Nothing wrong with that. I'd better tell you, though, that you're a little premature. It'll be a few months yet before we put any stock up for sale—probably not until after the first of the year."

"I'm in no hurry. Besides, I don't like to rush into an investment."

"Well, we appreciate your interest, in any case." Tedescu scraped through the clutter on his desk, came up with a package of filter-tipped cigars. He said as he lit one, "How acquainted are you with Mid-Pacific?"

"Not very. I understand you manufacture a component for industrial computers."

"Yes. A microcircuit. I could give you a technical rundown on it, but I'm afraid it wouldn't mean much to a layman."

"That's not necessary. Computer technology is big business these days; that's all I need to know."

"*Very* big business," Tedescu said. He clamped the cigar between his teeth. "We started on a shoestring five years ago; today we're on the verge of becoming a ten-million-dollar corporation. The sky's the limit in computer electronics, Mr. James."

"You have two partners, is that right?"

"Right. Phil Bexley and Carl Emerson."

"Emerson is the controlling partner?"

"Yes."

"I've been told he owns the patent on your microcircuit. Is he the one who designed it?"

Something happened in Tedescu's face, a subtle change as though strong emotion—anger or bitterness—had come up near the surface. "With my help, yes," he said. "The original concept was Carl's."

"You're a designer, too?"

"I am," he said, and the emotion was in his voice now. Just a trace of it, but enough to let me recognize it as bitterness.

"What about Bexley? What does he do?"

"Handles marketing and production."

"And Emerson?"

"Business development," Tedescu said. The bitterness was there again: he did not like Carl Emerson worth a damn, I thought. "I suppose you could say he's responsible for building Mid-Pacific into what it is today."

"The three of you own all the company stock, as things stand now?"

"Yes. Carl has fifty-one percent; Phil and I divide the balance."

"Why is that? I mean, why not three equal shares?"

Tedescu's eyes shifted away from me; he leaned forward to jab out his cigar in an onyx ashtray. "It was Carl's idea to form the company," he said. "The original microcircuit concept was his, as I told you, and he arranged to put up most of the money we needed to get started."

"Sounds as though he's pretty well off."

"He wasn't then, no. He had some capital from private investments and he managed to float a couple of loans through business contacts."

"What did he do before?"

"He was with Honeywell. So were Phil and I; that's how we met." Tedescu put his penetrating gaze on me again. "Are you always this curious, Mr. James?" he asked mildly.

"Just my nature, I guess. Do you mind my asking all these questions?"

He shrugged. "Not at all."

"Was it Emerson's idea to go public with your stock?"

"It was."

"For purposes of expansion?"

"That's right. We have patents pending on two new designs. All we need is sufficient capital to begin manufacture."

"Are the new designs also Emerson's?"

"No," Tedescu said, "they're mine."

"I see."

The smile he gave me seemed forced. "The fact is, we have a plant in Silicon Valley that we're in the process of expanding now." Silicon Valley was another name for Santa Clara County, a section of the Peninsula between Redwood City and San Jose where dozens of computer-related firms had established themselves in recent years. "Next year we hope to have a second plant, with a dozen new employees. And larger offices here in the city."

"Can you tell me how much stock you're planning to make available?"

"I'm afraid not. That decision hasn't been reached yet."

"But it'll be enough so that I can buy, oh, say a thousand shares?"

He raised an eyebrow. "That will be a substantial investment, you know."

"I think I can afford it. What will a share sell for?"

"I can't tell you that either. But a thousand shares will probably cost you a nice piece of change."

"From what you've told me, it would be well worth the risk."

"No question about that. Mid-Pacific will be a gold mine in a few years. A thousand shares could make you a rich man."

"That's good to hear," I said, but it wasn't. It wasn't good at all.

Tedescu glanced at his watch, my cue that the interview was finished. I took it; I'd got all I was going to get out of him. "Well, I've taken up enough of your time, Mr. Tedescu. Thanks for talking to me; I appreciate your candor."

"Not at all," he said. He was already on his feet. "My pleasure. I'll show you out."

He took me down the corridor and opened the door to the anteroom, and we shook hands again. I said, "I'll be waiting for an official announcement."

"Yes," he said. He sounded preoccupied now. "You do that, Mr. James."

He shut the door as soon as I was through it. Behind her desk, the secretary, Miss Addison, gave me another impersonal smile. I didn't answer it; I did not feel like smiling even to be polite.

Outside, the streets were crowded with office workers on their way to lunch. I wanted a cup of coffee and a place to do some quiet brooding, but all the coffee shops and lunch counters were jammed and I wasn't in a mood to share space with anybody. I made my way back to Montgomery, to the garage where I'd left my car. It was quiet in there, at least. I sat slumped on the car seat with my eyes closed, resting.

It looked bad for Eberhardt—very bad. Mid-Pacific was solvent and upwardly mobile, on the verge of major status in the computer industry; their stock, when they put it on the market, wouldn't come cheap, and would escalate rapidly in value if what Tedescu had told me was true. *A thousand shares could make you a rich man.* Yeah. A much more effective bribe than cash, a much more lucrative payoff— the kind that might tempt the most honest of men. Everybody has his price, so they say. You just don't know what it is until it's offered to you.

I kept trying to tell myself it wasn't that way, he hadn't gone over—not for any reason. But the evidence seemed damning; and I could not find another plausible explanation for the stock-transfer form in his safe. It made me feel dark inside, fed the anger, gave it a kind of hard focus. I was caught up in this thing now and I had to see it through, no matter that I no longer had an investigator's license, no matter what it cost me. It was personal. It was Eberhardt and the bribe angle and Mau Yee and the wound in my shoulder and the stiffened arm and a world full of injustice; it was everything, it was *me*. Until I got to the bottom of it, I could not get on with the business of putting my life back together. It was like a cancer that had to be cut out. Nothing else had any meaning until it was gone.

I stirred myself, straightened on the seat, and started the engine. There wasn't anything more I could do about Mid-Pacific Electronics and its three principals, not until after Ben Chadwick came up with the information I had asked him for. It was time to see what I could find out about Jimmy Quon. Time for a visit to Chinatown.

EIGHT

THERE WAS A LONG LINE of cars waiting to enter the Portsmouth Square garage, as there always was during the noon hour; it took me twenty-five minutes to get inside and deposit my car. The square itself was jammed with people, most of them elderly Chinese sitting on benches or playing cards or Oriental versions of checkers and dominoes on permanent concrete tables. I threaded my way through them, huddled inside my overcoat, and went up Washington to Grant Avenue.

The tourists were out in droves, despite the weather; there were more white faces along Grant than Chinese. The street, Chinatown's main thoroughfare, had undergone a cosmetic facelift in recent years. Everywhere you looked there was what the younger generation of Chinese referred to derisively as "pigtail architecture"—pagoda-style building facades, streetlamps, even public telephone booths, designed to give the tourists an "authentic" Chinese atmosphere. But Grant Avenue wasn't the real Chinatown; it was glitter and sham, a Disneyish version of Hong Kong or Canton, a visitors' enclave of souvenir shops, Chinese art and jade merchants, fancy restaurants, dark little bars. The real Chinatown was along Stockton and Kearny streets, in the back alleys and narrow streets on both sides of Grant. That was where you found the bundle shops, where seamstresses worked fourteen-hour days at their sewing machines for starvation wages; the tenements and projects;

the social clubs and gambling parlors and dingy Chinese theaters; the joss houses, the herb shops, the exotic groceries, the Chinese-language newspapers; the Chung Fat Sausage Company and the Golden Gate Fortune Cookie Factory and the First Chinese Baptist Church and the Chinese Cemetary Association and the ironically named Hang On Realty and Insurance. That was where you found the poverty, attitudes, and way of life that had changed remarkably little in over a century.

The address I had copied down for Kam Fong turned out to be on the block between Grant and Kearny, at the end of an alley not quite wide enough for two people to walk abreast. Six numbers, large enough to be read from the alley mouth on Jackson, were painted like graffiti on a board fence where the passage dead-ended. When I got to the fence I found a closed door in the right-hand wall, and when I opened that I was in another alley flanked on one side by doorways. The second doorway was the one I wanted. A pair of mailboxes were tacked up beside the door; neither of them bore a name. Under the boxes were doorbells, and I laid my thumb against each of them in turn.

Nothing happened inside. It was gloomy in the passage; not much light penetrated from above. It made me think of the old myth about a honeycomb of underground passageways beneath the streets of Chinatown, where sinister Orientals lurked and opium dens provided celestial dreams; even Hammett and his Continental Op had been guilty of perpetuating it. The myth had been born because a number of hidden, above-ground alleys like this one did exist, and in the days of the tong wars highbinders and hatchetmen had used them as escape routes from the police; the ignorant and the fanciful among the Caucasian population had reasoned, by illogical extension, that there was a similar subterranean network. The legend had been debunked decades ago, but myths, like dreams, die hard. There were still some, here and there, who believed it to this day.

I pressed the doorbells again. Pretty soon a window slid up above me, releasing a wave of cooking odors and the faint singsong of Chinese music from a radio or phonograph. I peered up past the metal framework of a fire escape at an elderly woman with a face like a wrinkled yellow grape.

She said something in Chinese, realized I was not of her race, and switched to heavily accented English. "What you want?"

"I'm looking for Kam Fong."

"Not here. Never here, noontime."

"Do you know where I can find him?"

"Restaurant, maybe."

"Which restaurant?"

"Mandarin Café. You try there."

"Where is it?"

"Kearny Street. Yes?"

"Yes," I said. "Thank you."

The wrinkled face withdrew and the window banged shut.

I went back out to Jackson, down to Kearny. It did not take me long to find the Mandarin Café; it was in the same block, over near Pacific—a hole-in-the-wall sandwiched between a barbershop and a Chinese dance studio. Inside was a long, narrow room crowded with tables and people, nearly all of them Chinese. They had the heat turned up in there, and combined with stove heat from the kitchen and body heat from the patrons, it gave the room an unpleasant tropical atmosphere spiced with the odors of mandarin cooking. The heat made sweat pop out on my forehead, made me feel vaguely nauseous. Nobody else seemed to mind it, but then none of them had just spent six days in the hospital recovering from a bullet wound.

I opened the buttons on my overcoat. While I was doing

that, a Chinese waiter came up and shook his head at me. "Sorry, no tables now. You wait?"

"I'm not here for lunch," I said. "I'm looking for a man named Kam Fong. You know him?"

"Kam Fong?"

"He lives around the corner on Jackson."

The waiter hesitated, and then shrugged and pointed toward the back of the restaurant.

"Which table?" I said. "I don't know what he looks like."

"Far corner. By kitchen door."

He went away. I squinted through the miasma of heat, picked up the table near the kitchen door, and made my way back there. It was a table for two, but Kam Fong was eating alone. He was a wizened little guy of indeterminate age, with a wispy mustache and glossy black hair and skin the color and appearance of tallow. He had a plate of fried pork and cabbage in front of him, and a big dish of rice and a pot of tea, and he was sitting hunched forward, working on his food with a pair of chopsticks and plenty of appetite. The meal had all of his attention; he didn't see me coming and he didn't look up until I pulled out the chair across from him and sat down.

"Kam Fong?" I said.

He looked blankly startled at first, but when he focused on me, saw the arm sling inside my open coat, his reaction was sudden and surprising. His mouth popped open, his eyes bulged, he made an odd little noise in his throat; one of the chopsticks slipped out of his fingers and clattered against the teapot. Fear, bright and shiny, spread like a flush over his waxy face.

"You," he said, and it came out half-strangled, like a belch.

I frowned at him. "You know who I am?"

"How you find me? How you know?"

I got it then. It was his voice; I'd heard it before. A spasm went through my left arm and I could feel the fingers twitch. In the space of a second I was as tense as he was.

"Well, well," I said. "You're the one who called yesterday to tell me about Mau Yee."

The mention of Mau Yee made him jerk as if I had slapped him. His fear flared up brighter; he looked around a little wildly, made a motion to get on his feet. I caught hold of his wrist with my good hand, put enough pressure on it to keep him sitting still.

"You're not going anywhere, Fong," I told him. "We're going to have a little talk, you and me."

"No, please . . ."

"Yes, please. Just take it easy, don't lose your head, and we'll get along fine."

He was wired up so tight you could almost see him quiver. I watched him struggle with his panic, try to get it under control. His eyes rolled around for three or four seconds; then he blinked, let out a heavy breath, and used his free hand to paw his mouth out of shape. He was all right, then. He wasn't going to make a scene.

"How you know?" he said again.

"I didn't know, not until you opened your mouth and I recognized your voice. I got your name from a mutual acquaintance."

"Who?"

"Inspector Richard Loo. He said you'd had some contact with Lieutenant Eberhardt in the past, given him information on certain matters. So I thought I'd look you up."

Fong wet his lips, slumped back a little in his chair. I still had hold of his wrist; when I released it he put both hands in his lap and glanced around again, furtively. But nobody was looking at us. They were all too busy eating and chattering among themselves.

"You telling them?" he asked. "Police?"

"About your call? No. I'm looking into things on my own."

That seemed to relieve him a little. "You not telling anyone? Not police, nobody in Chinatown?"

"That depends," I said. "On how cooperative you are, for one thing. Why did you call me?"

"Lieutenant, he . . ." The sentence dribbled off.

"What about the lieutenant?"

"He treat me okay. Not like other police."

"Paid you well, never hassled you?"

"Yes."

"And you called me because I'm his friend, because I was shot too."

"Yes."

"And because you heard he'd taken a bribe."

"Not want police to know," he said. "Maybe not true. I think maybe you find out."

"What do you know about this bribe?"

"Nothing. Only what I telling you before."

"No idea who's supposed to have given it?"

"No."

"But you know it wasn't a Chinese."

"No Chinese. Nobody in Chinatown."

"Where did you hear about the bribe?"

"I listen, hearing many things."

"Sure you do. Where did you hear this one?"

"Not remembering."

"You'd better start remembering, my friend. And quick."

He wet his lips again. "I think . . . Lee Chuck."

"Who would Lee Chuck be?"

"Herb seller. Important man."

"Yes? Does he have a shop?"

"Ross Alley."

"How did he know about the bribe?"

"He not telling me."

"What else does he do besides sell herbs?"

"Do?"

"Come on, Fong, you know what I mean."

Hesitation. Then he said, "Gambling."

"You mean he runs a parlor?"

"Yes."

"What kind?"

"Mah-Jongg, fan-tan, poker."

"High stakes?"

"Yes."

"Where?"

"Room above his shop."

"In Ross Alley?"

"Yes."

"Does the bribe have anything to do with gambling?"

"No."

"Then how does Chuck know about it?"

"He not telling me."

"Who told you about Mau Yee? Was it Chuck?"

"Yes."

"What did he say?"

Fong cast another furtive glance at the nearby tables. Then he leaned forward and lowered his voice a couple of octaves. "He saying Mau Yee try to eat two white pies. One big, one little."

"Meaning he tried to kill a couple of Caucasians."

"Yes. You and lieutenant."

"Why? What motive?"

"Something to do with bribe."

"But Chuck didn't say what."

"No."

"Did he have any idea who hired Mau Yee?"

"He saying no."

"Or why an outsider would want a Chinese gunman?"

"No."

"Why did Chuck tell you as much as he did?"

"We talk sometimes. Friends."

Some friends, I thought. "Does he belong to Hui Sip?"

"Yes. You know Hui Sip?"

"I've heard of them. What else do they control besides gambling? Drugs, maybe?"

"Yes."

"Uh-huh. Where can I find Mau Yee?"

"You go after him now?"

"I haven't decided that yet. Where does he live?"

"Hang Ah Street."

"What number?"

"Sixteen."

"Does he live there alone?"

"No. He having woman. Not married."

"All right," I said. I got my wallet out, took one of my business cards from inside. The telephone listed on it was my office number; I scratched that out with a pen and wrote my home number in its place. Then I slid the card over in front of him, next to his cold plate of fried pork and cabbage. "I need more information, Fong," I said. "I need to know who hired Mau Yee and why, what that bribe business is all about. See what else you can find out. You turn up anything positive, there'll be a hundred bucks in it for you."

He hesitated, finally picked up the card and put it into his shirt pocket. "Hearing nothing else," he said. "Only what Lee Chuck telling me."

"Nose around anyway. Maybe you'll get lucky."

"Yes." He leaned forward again. "You know Mau Yee carry puppy all time?"

"Puppy?"

"Pistol. All time different one—many puppies. You being careful, yes? Mau Yee very dangerous."

"So am I right now," I said.

The heat and the heavy cooking odors were making me a little dizzy. I pushed back my chair, got on my feet, told Fong I'd be in touch, and left him mopping his face with a linen napkin. When I got outside I leaned against a parking meter for a time, to let the wind cool me and chase away the dizziness.

Up on California, the bells were ringing in the steeple of Old St. Mary's. A wedding, probably. Or a funeral. The bells reminded me of the sign over the church entrance, underneath the big clock—a Biblical quote from Ecclesiastes. "Son," it said, "observe the time and fly from evil."

Good advice for most people, I thought, but not for me. Not now.

I had observed the time, all right, but I wasn't flying from evil; I was flying straight at it.

NINE

Ross Alley was a narrow thoroughfare between Jackson and Pacific, west of Grant Avenue. Lined with doorways that led to bundle shops, apartments, the headquarters of a couple of family associations; two sleazy-looking bars, one of which advertised "Belly Dance on Weekends"; several little shops with signs in Chinese calligraphy and opaque windows that hid their wares and their purpose from Caucasian eyes. Overhead, some of the buildings sported gilded pagoda cornices and there were fire escapes with fluttering laundry and hanging gardens and planters of black bamboo.

Halfway along I found a narrow storefront window decorated with Chinese characters and the words *Lee Chuck, Herbalist* in faded black. Inside, displayed on plates, were a dozen or so varieties of exotic herbs. Each of the plates had a piece of red paper stuck to it, identifying in English and Chinese what it contained: Old Mountain ginseng, cinnamon bark, Wu Hsi lizard tea, deer's horn, black fungus.

There were two doors set side by side in the alcove next to the window. One of them had a dusty glass pane and opened into the herb shop; the other one, hanging a little crooked in its frame, was solid except for a peephole at eye level. That one, I thought, would probably lead upstairs to the room where Lee Chuck ran his after-hours gambling parlor. I glanced up at the second story. Three windows, each with louvered green shutters drawn tight across it.

There would be blackout curtains on the inside, too, as an added precaution; and maybe a spotter stationed somewhere out here in the alley while the bigger games were in progress to warn against a possible police raid.

I opened the shop door and went inside to the accompaniment of a small tinkling bell. The interior was not much larger than the living room of my flat, fairly clean, lighted by three Chinese lamps. On the left was a counter, and behind that, across the entire wall, were blue-lacquered cabinets with hundreds of little drawers. At the rear, heavy bead curtains covered the entrance to an inner room. There was nobody in the front part of the shop, but a couple of seconds after I shut the door, the bead curtains parted and a man came through to meet me.

He was maybe sixty, average height, bald as an egg, wearing horn-rimmed glasses and Western-style clothes. If he was surprised to see a Caucasian in his shop, or if he had any idea of who I was, he didn't show it. Nothing changed in his bland expression or in the unblinking eyes behind his glasses. This guy was the stuff of stereotypes: the inscrutable Oriental.

"Yes?" he said politely. "May I help you?"

"Are you Lee Chuck?"

"At your service, sir. Have you an ailment?"

"Pardon?"

"That brings you to my humble shop. My tonics are all genuine, imported from China. Guaranteed effective for any ailment. You are familiar with Shen Nung, sir?"

"No," I said.

"The ancient father of plants. A thousand years ago, in old China, Emperor Shen Nung examined many plants to discover their medicinal value. His wisdom, like that of Confucius, has survived the centuries."

I wondered if he was putting me on. His tonics might have been genuine, but his patter was straight out of Charlie Chan. He might have mistaken me for a tourist and was serving up more stereotype, tongue-in-cheek, to go with his inscrutable look. Then again, he might have recognized me and was playing games to keep me off balance.

"I'm not here to buy herbs," I said. Then, to see if I could shake him a little, I gave him my right name and followed it by saying, "You know who I am, don't you, Chuck?"

It didn't buy me anything. His face remained impassive; there was not even a flicker of reaction in his eyes. He cocked his head to one side, birdlike, and said in the same polite voice, "I am afraid not, sir."

"Sure you do. My name has been all over the news lately. I got shot by a Chinese gunman eight days ago—me and a police lieutenant named Eberhardt."

He turned away from me, making it seem casual and unhurried, and went around behind the counter. He ran his hand over a section of the blue-lacquered cabinet, found a drawer a third of the way down. The fragrance of herbs was heavy in there, and it seemed to get even heavier when he opened the drawer.

"Some lizard tea, perhaps?" he said. "Most nourishing, a boon to the digestion."

"I heard there was some kind of bribe involved in the shooting," I said. "Maybe you know something about that."

Lee Chuck opened another drawer. "Mint leaves, sir? Excellent for combating fire in the human body."

"The man who did the shooting is known as Mau Yee. His real name is Jimmy Quon—a *boo how doy* for the Hui Sip tong."

Another drawer. "Ginseng, sir? Very fine. Ginseng soup, properly brewed, provides strength and a long life."

"You know Jimmy Quon, right? You're a member of Hui Sip yourself."

"Deer's tail from Hwei Chung? Like ginseng, it is one of mankind's greatest blessings."

"Upstairs," I said, "right over this shop, there's a gambling parlor. Fan-tan, Mah-Jongg, poker—high-stakes games. You run it for Hui Sip. The police might like to know about that."

"Sage tea? It also promotes a long life. And softens grief."

He was getting to me. The anger boiled up near the surface, and I had to fight off an impulse to reach over the counter and grab him by the neck. Violence would not have gotten me anything; Chuck was the kind who would absorb it stoically, without breaking, and then take his revenge later on. Like charging me with assault and battery, which was something I could not afford to have happen. My threat to tell the police about his game room upstairs didn't carry much weight. Gambling was only a misdemeanor; even if they shut him down for a while, he'd get off with a fine and be back in business inside a week.

"All right, Chuck," I said, "don't talk to me. But when you talk to Jimmy Quon, give him a message. Tell him I'm going to get him for what he did. Tell him if I have to I'm going to eat his pie."

"No herbs, sir? No fine tonics? There are more than one thousand prescriptions in the book of Li Shih-chen, the great physician of the Ming dynasty. Many would be of benefit, to assure you health and longevity."

"Don't give me any more of that crap. You want to threaten me, do it out in the open. Like I just threatened Jimmy Quon. Like I'm threatening *you*. If you're mixed up in what happened, I'll nail your ass too. That clear enough for you?"

Behind his glasses, his eyes were steady on my face. Snake's eyes: it seemed they hadn't blinked once the whole time I'd been there and they didn't blink now. "Are you familiar with Chinese folklore, sir?" he said. "Most interesting. We have sayings appropriate to all occasions. I am fondest of the one which states, 'Loud bark, no good dogs; loud talk, no wise man.' "

"There are a lot of Western sayings too," I said. "How about 'You're a long time dead?' Or maybe 'Shit or get off the pot?'"

"If you do not wish to buy my tonics, sir, I must humbly request that you leave my shop. I have prescriptions to fill for others more concerned with their well-being."

He didn't wait to see if I had anything else to say to him. He came out from behind the counter, in the same unhurried movements as before, and disappeared through the bead curtains. I had to curb another impulse to go after him. The fragrance of the herbs seemed overpowering now, like some sort of opiate affecting my sense of reason and control. Either I got out of there pretty quick or I was going to start busting the place up. And Lee Chuck along with it.

I backed to the door, yanked it open. The little bell tinkled musically, and that was more irritation; I had a mental image of myself ripping it off the wall. I went out and hurled the door shut behind me, hard enough to rattle the pane of glass and set the bell tinkling all over again.

A motorized ricksha, driven by a Chinatown tour guide and with a couple of tourists in the rear seat, was coming down the alley. I didn't see it right away and the damned thing almost ran me down. The driver yelled something at me; I yelled something back at him, a biological suggestion that brought shocked looks to the faces of the tourists. The three of them gaped at me as if they thought I might be a lunatic.

Well, maybe I was turning into one, at that. Maybe I was becoming unhinged. I had not handled Lee Chuck worth a damn; telling him what I knew, threatening him and Jimmy Quon, had been a stupid blunder. I admitted that as soon as I got myself calmed down. Now I was vulnerable, a walking target. Chuck would talk to Mau Yee, all right, and Mau Yee would come after me. He had tried to kill a cop; I had told Chuck I was looking for him and made it clear that I hadn't shared my knowledge with the police. Yeah, he'd come after me. He had no choice.

A damned fool, that was what I was. Running around like a pulp detective, getting in over my head. Jimmy Quon was half my age, he had two good arms, he was a professional thug. How the hell was I supposed to challenge him? He could make a move against me any time, anywhere. Crippled up the way I was, I would not stand half a chance of defending myself.

It's not too late to get out of it, I thought. Go talk to Marcus and Klein, tell them—

Tell them what?

I had no proof that Quon had shot Eberhardt and me. And he had a manufactured alibi, according to Richard Loo, that the police hadn't been able to shake. Tell them I had been withholding information? Tell them I had been chasing around the city, investigating an attempted homicide? They could throw me in jail for obstructing justice, for practicing without a license, while Quon and whoever had hired him got off scot-free. Tell them about the bribe thing, the stock-transfer form in Eberhardt's safe? If I did that, the media might get hold of it—and suppose Eb was innocent? A public flap would mark him for life, just as the one a few weeks ago had marked me.

No, damn it. Right or wrong, Jimmy Quon was my baby; I'd get him one way or another and I'd get the bastard who hired him, too. The hell with the risk. And the hell with the consequences.

I went up Washington, taking it slow because the hill there was steep, and cut through Spofford Alley and across Clay. Hang Ah Street was another narrow alley that opened off Clay and jogged through the block past the Chinese Playground. I seemed to recall that Hang Ah meant "old fragrance" and that the alley had been named after a long-vanished perfume factory founded by a German chemist. The fragrance it had these days was a lot less sweet: garbage, animal feces, cooking odors that came from the brick tenements surrounding the playground, that were piped through ventilators from the Hang Ah Tea Room at the opposite end.

I passed the offices of the *Young China Daily*, a couple of social clubs, and several doorways that led to tenement apartments. The door to Number Sixteen was painted green; the mailbox attached to it had no name on it. Public anonymity was a big thing among Chinatown residents. Even somebody as notorious as Mau Yee observed the custom of unmarked mailboxes.

Across from Sixteen were a row of benches and some spindly trees and a fenced-in section of tennis and volleyball courts. I sat sideways on one of the benches, looking up at the fire escape and the windows in Jimmy Quon's building. There was not much to see. The fire escape had a potted tree on it; some of the windows were shaded and some had curtains and one was open partway. A young woman moved around behind the open one, doing something I couldn't see. Quon's woman? I wondered if he was in there somewhere. I wondered if Lee Chuck had got in touch with him yet.

But I wasn't here to confront Mau Yee; that would have been another blunder. I just wanted to see where he lived, familiarize myself with the surroundings in the event I had to come looking for him here. So I did not stay long, just a couple of minutes. Then I got up and went back the way I'd come.

I would need to familiarize myself with Jimmy Quon, too, I thought as I headed down toward Portsmouth Square. As it was, I knew little enough about him; I didn't even know what he looked like. Kam Fong could supply a description and some information about his habits, but that could wait. There was something else I needed to do first, outside Chinatown. Something more important.

I needed to get myself a gun.

TEN

MILO PETRIE OPENED the door of his house in the Western Addition, saw me standing there on the porch, and said in surprised tones, "Jesus Christ, what're you doing here?"

He was a lean, hawk-nosed guy in his sixties, with plenty of spunk left in him—a retired patrolman who had spent most of his years on the force at the Ingleside Station. Nowadays he worked part-time as a security guard and field operative for private agencies like the one that used to be mine. He also had a collection of guns, and because I didn't own one myself, hadn't since I'd left the Department, he had let me borrow a handgun a time or two in the past for special jobs.

I said, "I need a favor, Milo."

"Yeah? How come you're not home in bed?"

"Why should I be home in bed?"

"Man, you just got out of the hospital. You shouldn't be out in weather like this."

"Don't worry about me," I said. "Can I come in?"

"Hell, yes, you can come in. You sure you're okay?"

"I will be if you've got some coffee."

"Always a pot on the stove."

He led me into the kitchen, pulled out a chair for me at the table, and poured coffee into a couple of mugs. "Wife's not here," he said as he handed me one. "Visiting relatives up in Oregon. That's where I was too, until Sunday; that's why I didn't come see you in the hospital. I didn't even hear about the shooting until three days after it happened."

I nodded, drank some of the coffee.

"Christ, what a rotten thing," Milo said. "You think Eberhardt's gonna make it?"

"He'll make it," I said.

"The boys have any idea who did it yet? Or why?"

"I don't think so."

"A Chinaman—that's one for the books. But they'll get him. A thing like this, a cop getting shot, they don't let up. You know that."

"Sure." The coffee was bitter, full of chicory; it warmed me, but it also irritated my stomach and reminded me that I hadn't eaten anything all day. "About that favor, Milo."

"Just name it," he said.

"I want to borrow a handgun."

He frowned. "What do you need a piece for?"

"Protection."

"From what?"

"I'd feel safer with it, that's all. I got shot once; I don't want it to happen again."

"You mean you think that Chinaman might come after you? I thought he was trying for Eberhardt and you just got in the way."

"That's how it was," I said. "But he might figure I had a better look at him than the Department let on. I don't want to take any chances."

Milo was silent for a time, watching me. Then he said, "You sure that's all it is?"

"What else would it be?"

"Like maybe you got ideas about hunting the Chinaman yourself. That wouldn't be smart."

"Milo, look, I want the gun for protection. You don't want to let me have one, just say so. I'll go somewhere else."

He watched me a while longer. "Okay," he said finally.

"I guess you know what you're doing. And you sure as hell got a right to protect yourself. What kind you want?"

"Thirty-eight Special. Same one I borrowed last time, if you still have it."

"I have it. The holster, too?"

"Yeah," I said. "I've still got my carry permit."

"Drink your coffee," he said. "I'll be right back."

He went away, and I drank the coffee and looked through the window into his backyard. There was a barbecue pit out there that reminded me of the one in Eberhardt's yard; I quit looking through the window.

Milo came back pretty soon, carrying the .38 tucked into its belt holster. When he gave it over to me he said, "It's loaded. You want any extra ammo?"

"If six rounds aren't enough, I won't be around to worry about extras."

"Well, I hope you don't have to use it."

"So do I," I said.

I declined his offer of another cup of coffee, said I would keep in touch, and got out of there. There was a chance he would report the loan of the gun, if he thought I was up to something, but I doubted it. Milo was the type to mind his own business. And even if he did report it, it wouldn't be a problem. I had a right to protect myself, just as he'd said, and nobody at the Hall was going to hassle me on that score.

It was after four by the time I entered my flat. I stripped off my overcoat and jacket and went into the bathroom. Wrapped inside the sling, my left arm was like something that no longer belonged to me, a prosthetic device where the arm used to be. The fingers were cramped up so that the hand resembled a claw; I could barely move them.

Cripple, I thought. One-armed bandit with a gun.

I went back into the bedroom and dialed Ben Chadwick's number in Hollywood. "I've got the information you wanted," he said. "Get yourself something to write with."

"Just a second." I rummaged around in the nightstand drawer, found a pen and a notepad, and then tucked the receiver between my chin and shoulder so I could write. "Okay, shoot."

"Carl Emerson. Thirty-seven Camelia Drive, Burlingame. Divorced, four years. Ex-wife's name is Jeanne Emerson; she lives in San Francisco, twenty-eight sixty Vallejo, apartment four-B. I figured you'd want her address too."

"I do. Does Emerson have a criminal record?"

"Not even a traffic citation."

"Uh-huh. Go ahead."

"Philip Bexley. Thirty-four nineteen North Point, San Francisco. Married, two children. One arrest, in 1969, for assault; charges dropped. Bar fight, no big deal."

"Got it."

"Orin Tedescu. Eighty Cypress Lane, Pacifica. Married, no children. Three arrests for drunk driving, all in the past four years, the latest one ten months ago; had his license suspended for half a year. Nothing else."

When I finished writing I asked, "Did you find out anything about Mid-Pacific Electronics?"

"Not much. Emerson, Bexley, and Tedescu own the company; you already know that. Successful outfit, respectable, no hint of anything going on under the table."

"Have any of the three got a sideline? Another business, anything like that?"

"I didn't turn it up, if so," Chadwick said. "But I didn't dig all that deep. You want me to do some more checking?"

"If you would."

"Sure. You're into me big in the favor department, you know that?"

"I know it. Just say the word if you need anything."

"Even though you don't have a license?"

[83]

"Even though I don't have a license."

"Call me tomorrow," he said. And added meaningfully, "If you're still out and around."

After we rang off I took another look at what he'd given me. Not much there, aside from the addresses. The link between one of those three men and Mau Yee, if there was a link, was buried. I still did not know enough even to speculate on what it was.

I went and got my notebook out of my coat and then dialed Kam Fong's number. Eight rings, no answer. The description of Jimmy Quon, the background data, would have to wait until tomorrow.

In the kitchen, I opened a can of soup and dumped it into a saucepan. While it was heating I set out some cheese and crackers, a package of mortadella, an overripe tomato. I didn't want any of it, but I kept telling myself I had to have the nourishment. The first few bites seemed to want to lodge in my throat; after that everything went down all right.

Fatigue had begun to drag at me, winding me down like an old clock. There were things I could do yet tonight, but the smart thing was to get into bed and rest. And the smart thing, after a not very smart day, was what I had better do.

Off the kitchen was a small utility porch; I went out there to make sure the back door, which opened onto a flight of stairs tacked onto the Victorian's side wall, and the porch windows were secure. Then I came back into the living room to put the chain on the front door and the lights out. Only I did not get a chance to do either of those things because in the hallway outside, somebody started scraping around in the door latch.

I stopped, tensing, and dragged the .38 out of its holster. The scraping sounds continued—either a key or a lock pick. I backed over toward the couch, half bent in the middle, with the gun out in front of me and my heart slugging away in my chest.

And the door opened and Kerry walked in.

When she saw me standing there with the gun she made a frightened bleating noise and dropped the ring of keys she had in her hand. "My God!" she said. "What are you *doing*?"

The tension fled all at once, leaving me limp. The .38 felt hot now, as if it had already gone off in silence, and my hand was shaking enough to make it wobble; I shoved it into the holster as I straightened up. On the carpet between us, the keys glinted in the room light. I had given her a key some time back; that was how she'd got into the building without buzzing from downstairs, how she'd got into the flat.

"Christ," I said, "I might have shot you. Why the hell didn't you ring the bell?"

"I thought you might be in bed. What's going on?"

"Nothing's going on."

"Why have you got that gun?"

Dull anger made my head pound. I moved around the couch and sat down, panting a little; something had gone wrong with my breathing. Kerry shut the door, bent to pick up the keys, and then came over and perched on the far side of the couch. She was no longer frightened, but her face was full of concern. The green chameleon eyes were almost black with it.

I said, "Why did you come here unannounced like that?"

"I wanted to see you. I drove straight over from work."

"You could have called first."

"I did call, twice this afternoon. You weren't here."

I didn't say anything.

"Answer my question," she said.

"What question?"

"About that gun. Why are you wearing a gun?"

"For protection," I said.

"Protection from what?"

"I got shot last week, remember?"

"And you think the gunman might come after you again? That's ridiculous. He wasn't after you, he was after Eberhardt."

"You don't know that for sure. Neither do I."

"Is that who you thought I was? The gunman?"

"What else was I supposed to think? I wasn't expecting you. I told you I'd call when I was ready to see you again."

"I don't believe you," she said. "There's something else going on, something you're hiding."

I was still having trouble with my breathing. Hyperventilation, maybe. I lay my head against the back of the couch and made myself take air in slow inhalations through my mouth.

Kerry said, "Will you please, for God's sake, tell me what's happening!"

"No. There's nothing to tell."

"You think I'm blind? Look at you: you're exhausted, you're tense, you're white as a sheet. You've been acting funny for days, you went out somewhere yesterday and you were gone all day today. And now you're wearing a gun. I may not be a detective, but I can figure out what all of that means."

My lungs were working better now. I lifted my head and looked at her. "Can you?"

"You're hunting that gunman," she said.

"No, I'm not."

"I think you are. What I can't understand is why. Vengeance, is that it? Some sort of crazy vendetta?"

"No."

"If you find him, then what? Will you shoot him down in cold blood?"

"I'm not a killer. Is that what you think?"

"I don't know what to think anymore."

"Then don't think anything. Let me take care of myself."

"But you're not taking care of yourself, that's the point.

What if the police find out what you're doing? What if they find out you're carrying that gun?"

"I've got a permit for the gun," I said.

"They could put you in jail for interfering with a police investigation. You know that as well as I do."

"Nobody's going to put me in jail."

"Or else you'll wind up right back in the hospital," she said. "Don't you care about your health?"

"I care about it. I care about a lot of things."

"Including me?"

"You don't have to ask that question."

"Then why won't you confide in me? Why won't you listen to reason?"

"Kerry, look, I know what I'm doing. I've got reasons."

"What reasons?"

"I can't tell you right now."

"Why can't you?"

"Because I can't. Let it go at that, will you?"

"I don't want to let it go. Don't you see that I care about you too? More than I ever did—more than I was willing to let myself believe the past few weeks. It can be good for us again; we can start over, we can move ahead, we can have a future. Isn't that what you want?"

"You know it is."

"But you're not letting it happen. The shooting, Eberhardt in a coma . . . it's monstrous. But something good can come out of it; it can bring us back together, if only you'd let it."

"I will let it."

"When?"

"When this thing is over."

She pursed her lips. "It might be too late then."

"It won't be. I'll be all right."

"Will you? I don't know if I will be. I don't know if I'll still want you then—a man with secrets, a man who carries a gun. The man I want is the one you used to be, not the one you are now."

"Kerry, I love you. Isn't that enough?"

She was leaning toward me, with one hand spread on the cushion in front of her. I reached out to touch it, but she moved it away. "I'm not sure," she said. "Maybe it isn't."

"Try to understand. This is something I have to do. I couldn't walk away from it now if I wanted to. And the less you or anyone else knows about it, the better."

"Why? Because it might get you killed?"

"Because it's something I have to handle alone."

"All right," she said stiffly. "Have it your way." The ring of keys was still in her hand; she took mine off it, laid it on the coffee table. "Here's your key. So you won't have to worry about me coming back uninvited."

"You don't have to do that—"

"You don't have to do what you're doing either." She stood. "I'd better go."

"Are you sure you don't want to stay a while longer?"

"Yes, I'm sure. It wouldn't do either of us any good."

"I guess maybe not."

"I won't bother you again," she said. "Call me if you want to talk, or if you decide to come to your senses."

She crossed to the door, opened it, looked around at me as if she thought I might change my mind and call her back. I just sat there. It was a hard thing to do; I loved her, and maybe she loved me and was ready to give me another chance, and I hated this new crisis between us. But the other thing was in the way, like a wall I had to knock down before I could get to her or back to myself. There was no way to explain it, no way to make it any different. That was just the way it was.

"If I have to go to your funeral," she said from the doorway, "I won't cry. I just want you to know that." And then she was gone.

I sat in silence for a time. I could feel the gun digging into my side—that damned gun. You could have shot her, I thought. Who the hell do you think you are, Mike Hammer? The wild-eyed crusader, the vigilante with a gun and a "get them before they get us" philosophy? Borderline lunatic stuff. Don't let it happen, brother. Do what you have to do, but don't cross that line.

After a while I got up and put the chain on the door and took myself into the bedroom. I was asleep as soon as I flopped into bed.

ELEVEN

THE TELEPHONE woke me.

It was dark in the room, but I had not been asleep very long; I came up out of it groggy and disoriented, with a kind of bloated feeling, the way you do after you've been wrenched out of a deep sleep after only a few hours. When I struggled over toward the phone I came down hard on my left shoulder; pain rocketed the length of the arm, brought a strangled yell out of me. But it also cleared away some of the sticky web in my mind. I twisted back the other way, gritting my teeth, and kicked the wadded sheets out of the way and heaved into a sitting position.

The phone kept on ringing as I squinted at the night-stand clock. Ten-fifteen; I had been out close to four hours. I hauled up the receiver in the middle of another jangle and muttered a hello.

A male voice—a Chinese voice—said, "This is Jimmy Quon."

That woke me up all the way. I took a tighter grip on the receiver and started to say something, but the words got caught in the dryness caking my throat. I worked up saliva, swallowed it, and this time I got the words out.

"What do you want, Quon?"

"I hear you looking for me. I think we better talk."

"So talk. I'm listening."

"Not on the phone. You want to meet me?"

"Why should I meet you?"

"That's what you want, right? Face to face?"

"When?"

"Right now. You say where."

"Sure. And you show up with that three fifty-seven Magnum of yours."

"I got no big puppy like that, man," he said. "You wrong about me; I didn't have nothing to do with the dogs barking at you and the cop."

"No, huh?"

"No. But maybe I know who did. You want to meet or not?"

"Yeah. I'd like a good look at you, sonny."

"Pick a place. Public as you want."

"St. Francis Hotel, lobby bar. Forty-five minutes."

"Okay. I'll be there."

"Alone, Quon. And unarmed. Don't try anything with me."

"In a place like the St. Francis? Hey, I told you, man, you wrong about me. I don't throw dog feed at the *fan quai.*"

"Forty-five minutes," I said, and hung up on him.

I switched on the bedside lamp, used part of one sheet to wipe mucus out of my eyes. So what the hell is this? I thought. Some kind of trap, maybe, but I couldn't see how it would work. He'd let me pick the place, and he'd have to be crazy to try taking me out in the lobby of the St. Francis; it was a highly respectable hotel on Union Square, always crowded, with a good security force. He could try it on the street outside, either before or after the meeting, but the streets in that area were well populated and well patrolled. Besides which, the St. Francis had three entrances on three different streets; he had no way of knowing which one I would use.

There were a hundred better, safer ways to make his move against me, and none of them required a telephone call to set up a meeting. It was possible that he'd been telling the truth, that he *wasn't* the body-washer who'd gunned down Eberhardt and me—but if that was the case, then why had Kam Fong lied to me? Why had Lee Chuck put on his Charlie Chan act and made his veiled threats? No, I didn't buy it. Quon was the boy, all right. And he was up to something. But what, damn it? What was the purpose in announcing himself to me beforehand?

In the bathroom, I ran cold water into the sink and washed my face. Then I got myself dressed and presentable enough so I could walk into the St. Francis without causing a stir. When I had the .38 clipped on under my jacket I shrugged one-armed into my overcoat, put on a hat to keep my head warm, and went out and double-locked the door behind me.

There was fog mixed with the overcast now, but it was a high fog, capering over the tops of the buildings. The street and the sidewalks were empty at the moment; they glistened faintly in the shine of the streetlamps and building lights. I turned left off the stairs, toward where I had parked my car. The wind blew chill against my face; crosscurrents of it came down the narrow, cement-floored alley that separated my building from the one adjacent, tugging at my hat, and I reached up to jam the thing down a little tighter on my head.

And that was when I saw the dark-colored sedan illegally parked in one of the driveways next door.

The sedan was the first warning. The second was the shadowy presence on the passenger side, and the third and fourth were the facts that the window was rolled down and the door was not quite shut. All the muscles in my body seemed to knot up at once. I did not have time to think; the rest of it was instinct. I was already moving, sweeping the flaps of my overcoat and jacket back so I could get at the .38, when he came up out of the car. And I was two steps into the blackness of the alley before he cut loose with his first shot.

The gun made a muffled farting sound—not the .357

Magnum, a smaller piece outfitted with a silencer; the slug missed somewhere behind me and there was a thwacking undersound as it buried itself in the side wall of my building. I couldn't see where I was going; my right knee hit something—one of the garbage cans tucked back in there —just as I yanked the .38 free of its holster. It broke my stride, made me stumble. Then I banged into another of the cans, got my feet tangled up, and went down in a sideways sprawl that clacked my teeth together and caused an eruption of pain in my shoulder.

The fall probably saved my life. A second bullet slashed at the air above me; I heard the whine of a ricochet off one of the metal storage bins at the rear of the alley. I still had a grip on the .38. I scrambled around with it on the rough floor, amid a thin litter of wind-blown leaves and papers, until I was lying extended on my right side, facing toward the street. Pain and sweat had blurred my vision, but I could see him out there on the sidewalk, outlined by the streetlamp across the way—feet spread, body dipped into the same kind of shooter's crouch he'd used at Eberhardt's house.

He squeezed off a third time before I could get him lined up. It was a low shot, wide again; the slug burned off the pavement, skipped away into the blackness. One of my legs jerked in involuntary reflex and the shoe heel cracked into another garbage can. The lid came off, hit the pavement with an echoing clatter just as I pulled the trigger on the .38.

The shot was wild, like all of his had been, but the fact that I was armed and all the sudden noise made him unwilling to stick around for any more gunplay. He dodged away from the alley, back to where the sedan was. I levered up to my knees, grunting with the effort, and swiped the sweat out of my eyes with the coat sleeve. Above and behind me, somebody started yelling; it sounded like my neighbor, Litchak. Out on the street, the sedan's engine roared. I made it to my feet as the car cut into view, tires howling, headlights dark. It seesawed out into the middle of the street, straightened out, and was gone before I could take more than three stumbling steps toward the alley mouth.

I stopped; I had nowhere to go now, no way to give chase. And a flashlight beam had come on and was poking down around me: Litchak. The gun, I thought, don't let him see it. I jammed it into the holster, pulled the coat and jacket flaps over it an instant before the cone of light picked me up.

"What the hell is going on down there?"

I turned into the glare of the flash. Litchak was up on the staircase landing outside his back door, leaning over the railing with the flashlight at arm's length. When he recognized me he called something I could not make out and came thumping down the stairs. In the adjacent building, a couple of people had their heads poked out of open windows, gawking. I glanced back at the street again, but there wasn't anybody out there that I could see.

My shoulder felt as though somebody had set it afire; I could not move the arm at all without aggravating the pain. I was breathing in little ragged gasps when Litchak pounded up.

"I should've known it would be you," he said. He was wearing bathrobe and slippers, and what hair he had stuck up at angles like a fright wig. "Christ Almighty, what'd you get yourself into this time?"

"It's nothing," I said. "Forget it."

"Yeah? I thought I heard a shot."

"No. Nothing like that."

"Well then? What was all the commotion about?"

"Kids," I said. "They hassled me a little, that's all. Tried to muscle me around back here as I was leaving the building."

"You want me to call the cops?"

"No," I said. "I told you, it's nothing important."

He didn't believe me; that was plain enough even in the darkness. But he didn't press it. He knew me pretty well— he'd been peripherally involved in a couple of my past skirmishes—and he was the kind, like Milo Petrie, who minded his own business.

He said, "You hurt? You don't look so good."

"Banged up my bad shoulder. I'll be okay."

"Sure?"

"Positive. Go on back to bed."

The people in the adjacent building were still gawking out of their windows; I called up to them to go to bed too, there was nothing more to see and nothing to worry about. I did not want anybody over there calling the police, either.

"You better hit the sack yourself," Litchak said, "the shape you're in."

"I will. I shouldn't have come out in the first place."

"I guess you shouldn't. I never saw a man like you. You attract trouble like that garbage over there attracts flies. You don't watch yourself, my friend, you'll wind up in a coffin before your time."

"Yeah," I said.

He went back up the side stairs, shaking his head, and I went out to the street. My hat was lying on the sidewalk; I stooped to pick it up. Then I went in through the front entrance and upstairs to my flat. I was all right until I got inside; then delayed reaction set in, as it always does after a thing like this, and I had a few bad minutes—the shakes, hot and cold flashes, stomach cramps. I stayed in a chair, not thinking about anything, enduring it, until my brain and my body quieted down.

The fire still burned in my shoulder. I went into the bathroom, washed the grit from the alley off my hands and face. Then I stripped off my clothes and removed the bandage and looked at the wound. It had an inflamed look around the edges and one of the remaining stitches had pulled loose. Not too bad, though, considering; I could have ripped the whole thing wide open. I was due for a visit to Doctor Abrams tomorrow—he could take care of it then. I did not want to put anything on it myself because I didn't know if that was the right thing to do.

I put the bandage back on and went and got into bed. The fingers on my left hand were cold as well as stiff; I lay there massaging warmth into them. Thinking about Jimmy Quon.

The way he had worked his trap was so damn simple I hadn't even considered it. Set up a phony meeting just to get me out of the building at a certain time, so he could ambush me out front. He could not have known I would be in bed when the call came, that it would take me a few minutes to get dressed and moving; I could have left immediately after the call. Which meant the voice on the phone hadn't belonged to him. He would not have had time to talk to me, even from down on Van Ness or somewhere else nearby, and then get up here and into position. No, it had to have been some friend of his, maybe another *boo how doy* for Hui Sip. I'd never heard Quon's voice; if the caller said he was Jimmy Quon, I was supposed to believe it. And I had, pretty as you please.

Stupid. Stupid! Two major blunders today, and the second one in spite of my vows to use my head, be careful, not make any more mistakes. I had been lucky this time, but if I let it happen again, the odds were I'd be dead. And Kerry could keep her promise not to cry at my funeral.

Getting old, getting slow, getting stupid—yeah. But there wouldn't be any third blunder. Quon wasn't going to kill me; no way. He'd had his chance tonight and he'd blown it, and now it was my turn. Now I was the one who was going to eat some pie.

Mau Yee, I thought, you're a dead cat. One way or another, sooner or later—a dead cat.

TWELVE

NIGHTMARES PLAGUED my sleep—blood and shadow, guns flashing, Chinese faces leering at me with Cheshire cat smiles out of a dark and bloody sky—and I woke up twice, drenched in sweat. But except for the dull ache in my shoulder, the same paralysis in the arm and hand, I was in fair enough shape in the morning.

I took a couple of the Empirin-and-codeine tablets Abrams had given me, and then brewed some coffee and made myself eat a couple of eggs and a piece of toast. It was a few minutes before nine when I left the flat, wearing the .38 and a different overcoat because the one I'd had on last night was soiled and had a rip in one sleeve. When I got downstairs, I scanned the street through the door glass before I stepped outside. I doubted if Jimmy Quon would come after me again right away, in broad daylight, but I had plenty of reason to be paranoid. I also opened the hood on my car to check the engine, and felt around under the dash when I got inside. For all I knew, Mau Yee was as handy with bombs as he was with his puppies.

Nobody followed me as I drove down to the Marina District; I made sure of that, too. The North Point address Chadwick had given me for Philip Bexley turned out to be a private house near the Palace of Fine Arts. It had been newly painted, and there were a couple of strips of lawn and some flowering shrubs in front. There were also an iron grillwork gate across the porch and grillwork bars over the first-floor windows. Everybody in the city had a reason to be paranoid these days.

I found a place to park a few doors away. In the glove compartment was an envelope with an accumulation of business cards people had given me; I rummaged around in there until I came up with one that said: *North Coast Insurance Company—Lloyd Rable, Claims Representative.* I put the card into my coat pocket and then got out and locked the car and walked back to the Bexley house.

It took a minute or so for somebody to answer the doorbell. A cold wind, damp with fog, chilled my neck and ears as I waited; I'd forgotten to wear my hat today. When a chain finally rattled inside and the door opened I was looking at the beefy guy I had run into outside the Mid-Pacific offices yesterday. He was wearing a different three-piece suit, expensively cut, and he had a briefcase under one arm.

He remembered me, too; recognition formed a row of frown lines between his eyebrows. I hadn't expected him to still be home—it was his wife I'd figured to talk to—and the question now was, did he know who I was? He did if he was the man behind Jimmy Quon. Or if he'd seen my photograph in the papers and made the right connection. The other possibility was that Orin Tedescu had mentioned my talk with him, in which case I would have to keep on being Andrew James.

He said, "Yes? What is it?" in a neutral voice.

Go slow, I thought, play it by ear. "Mr. Bexley?"

"That's right."

"I saw you yesterday morning, didn't I? Outside your offices? I was just getting out of the elevator and you were just getting on."

"Yes, I remember."

"I'm sorry to have missed you then," I said. "But I did spend a few minutes with Mr. Tedescu. Perhaps he mentioned me?"

"No, I didn't go back to the office yesterday. What is it you want?"

That took care of Andrew James. And if Bexley had any idea of my real identity, he wasn't letting on; which might mean he was willing to play games, to see what I was up to. So I said, "My name is Lloyd Rable," and took the business card out of my pocket and handed it to him through the gate. "North Coast Insurance."

He looked at the card, still frowning. The bars made it seem as though one of us was in a cage. At length he put his eyes on me again; the only expression in them was one of polite disinterest. "I'm not in the market for any insurance," he said.

I gave him a toothy smile. "No, no, that's not why I'm here. I'm a staff investigator, not a sales agent. The head of your company, Mr. Emerson, has applied for a rather large policy with us. He gave your name as one of his references. I'd like to ask you a few questions about him, if you wouldn't mind."

"What sort of questions?"

"Oh, on his background, habits, financial status, things like that. Mostly for purposes of confirming data he supplied on his application. It's standard procedure when an individual applies for a substantial policy."

"Well . . . I was just on my way to the office. I'm already late as it is."

"I won't take up much of your time, Mr. Bexley. And it would save my having to bother you again later on."

He thought it over. Or seemed to. Pretty soon he shrugged and said, "All right. I guess I can give you ten minutes."

"I'd appreciate it."

Bexley unlocked the gate and showed me into a spacious living room outfitted with blond furniture and at least three dozen house plants that gave the room a greenhouse atmosphere. Somewhere at the rear of the house, kids were making noise. A woman's voice yelled at them to be quiet. I sat down on the couch, and while I was getting out my notebook the woman appeared in a doorway. She was blond like the furniture, attractive in a gaunt way, wearing a pink housecoat and fuzzy pink mules.

"Who is it, Phil?" she asked.

"This is Mr. Rable," Bexley told her, gesturing toward me. "He's an insurance investigator. He wants to ask me some questions about Carl."

"Oh," she said, "Carl," and her mouth got a little pinched at the corners. "Is he in some sort of trouble, I hope?"

"No. He just applied for some insurance, that's all."

The woman looked disappointed. "I'm sorry to hear that. If he was in trouble, it would have made my day."

"Linda," Bexley said sharply, "why don't you go do something about those boys? It sounds like they're tearing up the bedroom back there."

"They're just playing—"

"I don't care what they're doing. Get them quieted down, will you?"

She made a face and muttered something I didn't catch; but she went away. Bexley sat in an armchair across from me. There was a cut-glass cigarette box on the table next to him; he got a filtertip out of there and lit it with a table lighter.

I said, "Your wife doesn't seem to care much for Mr. Emerson."

"I guess she doesn't."

"May I ask why?"

"Personal reasons."

"Do you feel the same way?"

"Carl and I get along all right."

"Would you consider him a friend?"

"Not really. A business associate."

"How long have you known him?"

"Six years. He was with Honeywell when I went to work there; that's how we met."

"How would you describe him generally?"

"High-powered," Bexley said without hesitation. There were traces of bitterness in his voice, just as there had been in Orin Tedescu's yesterday. "When he makes up his mind to do something he goes out and does it. On his terms. He doesn't let anything or anybody stand in his way."

"That sounds as though he might be a little unscrupulous."

"I wouldn't go that far. He—"

The woman's voice rose again from the rear bedroom. One of the kids quit yelling, but the other one kept it up in an argumentative way. Then he broke off and let out a howl, as if the woman had smacked him one, and began to cry noisily.

Bexley winced. "Kids," he said. "You have any?"

"No. I'm not married."

"They get on your nerves sometimes." He made a meaningless gesture with his cigarette. "What was I saying?"

"That you wouldn't call Mr. Emerson unscrupulous."

"No, I wouldn't. Not exactly. I don't want you to get the wrong impression; he hasn't done anything unethical in building up our firm. Mid-Pacific is aboveboard in every way, Mr. Rable. Orin Tedescu and I see to that."

"Meaning Mr. Emerson might do something unethical if you weren't around?"

"No, I don't want to imply that either."

I made a couple of squiggles in the notebook, just for show. Bexley watched me write with the book balanced on one knee, and when I looked up again he asked, "What happened to your arm?"

"An accident."

"Car accident?"

"Yes. Even insurance investigators have them now and then."

He smiled sympathetically. "Must be difficult, trying to do things with one hand."

"It is," I said. "Can you tell me if Mr. Emerson has ever been in trouble?"

"Trouble? You mean with the law?"

"With anyone at all."

"No, I don't think so."

"Lawsuits, anything like that?"

"No."

"What about his personal life?"

A little boy about five or six came running into the room; his face was scrunched up, wet with tears. "Daddy, she hit me!" he wailed. "Mommy *hit* me!"

"Oh, for God's sake," Bexley said. He glanced at me, said, "Excuse me a second, will you?" and got up and scooped the little boy into his arms and carried him out of the room.

I looked around at the potted plants. It's not Bexley, I thought. He wasn't putting on an act for my benefit; the things he'd said so far, the domestic stuff, had the feel of authenticity. Unless I was losing my sense of judgment, he was just a guy with a wife and a couple of kids and a thinly veiled dislike for one of his business partners.

I listened to muffled voices and then silence as the little boy stopped crying. Bexley came back and sat down again and said, "Sorry about that. I had to play peacemaker."

"No problem."

He lit another cigarette; he'd got rid of the other one while he was out of the room. "You were asking me about Carl's personal life, right?"

"Yes."

"Well, I'm not sure I ought to talk about that. He wouldn't like it if he found out."

[102]

"He won't find out, Mr. Bexley. These interviews are strictly confidential."

"Yes? Do you mind telling me if Mr. Tedescu talked freely when you interviewed him?"

"He was very cooperative, yes."

"I'll bet." Bexley's mouth quirked into a sardonic smile. "I'm surprised Carl listed him as a reference."

"Why is that?"

"They've had their differences in the past."

"Over business matters?"

"Primarily."

"Would you care to elaborate?"

"I'd rather not. It doesn't have anything to do with what we're discussing here." He paused. "Just what sort of policy did Carl apply for, anyway? Life insurance?"

"Yes. Property insurance as well, on his home in Burlingame."

"May I ask who's the beneficiary on the life policy?"

"I'm not at liberty to divulge that."

"Sorry. I was just curious. Carl doesn't have any relatives, and it certainly wouldn't be Tedescu or me. Or his ex-wife."

"Do you know his ex-wife?"

"Just to talk to. I haven't seen her since the divorce."

"What was the reason for it? The divorce, I mean."

He shrugged. "Carl never said. But it wasn't an amicable split, I can tell you that. Not the way he acted after it happened."

"How did he act?"

"Oh, angry and upset. The divorce was her idea, not his; he didn't seem to want it."

I nodded. "How would you characterize Mr. Emerson's present life-style?"

"I really can't answer that question."

"No? Why is that?"

"He keeps his private life pretty much to himself."

"You don't socialize with him?"

"No. An occasional business dinner, that's about it. We've never been to his house, he's never been to ours. As I said before, my relationship with him is strictly business."

"I see."

"Yes," Bexley said.

"Can you tell me anything at all about his habits?"

"What do you mean by habits?"

"Well . . . does he use drugs, for instance?"

"Why do you want to know that?"

"Drug users are health risks," I said.

"Really?" Bexley said, as if he didn't believe it. "Well, I wouldn't be surprised if he smokes a little grass. Who doesn't, these days?"

I didn't. But I said, "Hard drugs of any kind?"

"Not that I know of."

"How about women?"

"Women? You mean is he a swinger?"

"Yes."

"I suppose he gets his share. But he doesn't talk much about it."

"Is there any vice he might have that he does talk about?"

"Just one. And not much about that, either."

"What would that be?"

"Gambling," Bexley said. "It's a big passion with him."

I sat up a little straighter. "What sort of gambling?"

"You name it. Horses, football games, blackjack, craps. And poker—especially poker."

"Does he play for high stakes?"

"I wouldn't be surprised. He usually wins, too. Or he does to hear him tell it."

"Is there any place in particular he goes for poker?"

"Las Vegas. Three or four times a year."

"How about here in the city?"

"None that he's ever mentioned."

There it is, I thought, the possible connection. Carl

Emerson is a heavy gambler; Lee Chuck runs a gambling parlor for the Hui Sip tong; Jimmy Quon is a body-washer for Hui Sip. But Emerson was a Caucasian, and those Chinatown parlors were generally reserved for Chinese gamblers. How would Emerson get in on high-stakes games at Lee Chuck's? Why would he want to, given the fact that there were plenty of other gambling spots in San Francisco?

I could not think of a way to pump more information out of Bexley without making him suspicious. And I didn't want to blow my cover; Bexley may not have liked Emerson much, but if he realized I wasn't who I said I was, it might drive him straight to his partner to find out what was going on. If Emerson *was* the man behind Jimmy Quon, I did not want him to know I was on to him. There were others who might be able to tell me if Emerson and Lee Chuck were connected. Kam Fong, for one. Emerson's ex-wife, for another.

I said, "Has Mr. Emerson ever lost enough gambling to put him in financial difficulty?"

"If he has, he's kept it to himself."

"Then as far as you know, he's financially solvent?"

"As far as I know. That ranch he bought up in Mendocino County didn't come cheap."

"Ranch?"

"You don't know about that?"

"No. There was no mention of it on his application."

"Place called Seaview Ranch, somewhere near Mendocino. The village, I mean. Carl bought it about six months ago—his weekend retreat, so he says."

"An expensive piece of property?"

"I don't know what he paid for it, but you can't buy real estate anywhere in California these days without shelling out a good piece of change for it."

"True enough. Is there anything else you can tell me about Mr. Emerson that my company ought to know?"

"I can't think of anything, no." Bexley consulted his watch. "I have an appointment at eleven; I can just make it if I leave now. If you don't have any more questions, Mr. Rable . . ."

"I think that's about it," I said. I put the notebook and pen away, and when I stood up Bexley did the same.

He said, "I'd like to ask *you* a question."

"Go right ahead."

"Are Carl's policy applications going to go through?"

"That's not up to me. I'm just a field investigator."

"But you do recommend acceptance or denial?"

"In some cases, yes."

"What I've just told you . . . will it have a bearing on your recommendation in this case?"

"It might. I still have other people to see."

"Well, I hope I've been of some help," he said.

"You have, and I appreciate it."

"My pleasure." He smiled at me. There was a kind of satisfaction in the smile, as if he thought maybe he'd said enough to turn me against Emerson and the prospect pleased him. "If you'll just wait while I say good-bye to my wife, I'll walk out with you."

"Fine."

He disappeared again into the back of the house, and after a moment I heard him talking to Mrs. Bexley. The North Coast Insurance card was on the table next to his armchair, where he'd put it when he sat down; I moved over there and picked it up and slipped it into my pocket. I was standing by the door when Bexley returned. He didn't even look at the table as he caught up his briefcase.

Outside, he shook my hand and gave me another smile before he went to open his garage. He was in a much better mood than when I'd arrived. I may not have made his wife's day, but I had sure made Bexley's.

Now, I thought as I walked to my car, let's see if somebody can make mine.

THIRTEEN

TWENTY-EIGHT SIXTY Vallejo Street turned out to be an old brick apartment building at the foot of Russian Hill, just above the Broadway tunnel. The bank of mailboxes on the porch confirmed that Jeanne Emerson lived in 4B, but there was no answer when I pushed the doorbell next to her nameplate. It figured she had a job somewhere, being divorced, which meant she probably wouldn't be home until later in the day. I could have canvassed her neighbors to find out where she worked, but it seemed a better idea to wait. I wanted to talk to her in private; people are much more apt to be candid in their own homes than in their places of business, particularly when you were trying to get them to discuss their personal lives.

I drove through the tunnel to Montgomery and then swung around to Portsmouth Square. By the time I got into the garage and parked the car, it was almost eleven-thirty. From a phone booth I called Leo Vail at Waller & Company, identified myself as Andrew James, and asked him what else he'd been able to find out about Mid-Pacific Electronics.

"Not much, I'm afraid," he said. "As I indicated to you yesterday, they're quite a successful firm already and promise to be even more successful once they expand. Of course, a lot depends on their methods of expansion; they could be too ambitious, get in over their heads. But on the face of it, I think I can recommend purchase once their stock goes on sale."

"What about Carl Emerson?" I asked. "I've done some checking on my own and I understand he's something of a reckless sort."

"If that's the case," Vail said, "your sources are better than mine. As far as I've been able to determine, Emerson and his partners have built Mid-Pacific on sound, shrewd business acumen."

"Well, it doesn't really matter. I've pretty much made up my mind to go ahead in any case." I thanked him again, told him I would be in touch when Mid-Pacific made their official announcement, and hung up before he could ask me for an address and a telephone number.

There were fewer people in Portsmouth Square today, because of the fog and the raw wind off the bay. I cut through there to Grant Avenue. It gave me an odd feeling to be back in Chinatown, after what had happened yesterday and last night; I kept thinking this or that Chinese was looking at me as I passed, as if I wore some sort of brand that marked me as an enemy. Paranoia again. But the .38 on my belt was a reassuring weight just the same.

On Jackson, I walked down the narrow alley and into the passageway to Kam Fong's door. But he wasn't home today either; the same old woman stuck her head out of the same second-floor window and told me that in her broken English. Which left another visit to the Mandarin Café. If that was Fong's regular noonday haunt, it was a good bet I'd find him there; my watch said that it was almost twelve.

Because it was still early, the Mandarin was only three-quarters full. I scanned the patrons from just inside the door; Fong wasn't among them. There was an empty table along the near side wall, and I went over there and sat down to wait. I had nowhere else to go. If he didn't show up by one o'clock, I would have to go back and camp on his doorstep; but that was something to worry about if and when the time came.

When one of the waiters came around I ordered a pot of tea and a bowl of soup. It was too warm in there again; I shrugged out of my overcoat. That made the arm sling even more prominent, and once more I had the feeling that some of the Chinese customers were giving me covert looks. Cut it out, I told myself. They're just people. There's no sinister alliance among the Chinese population; that's a lot of racial crap and you know it. The only Chinese you've got to worry about are Jimmy Quon and his pals in Hui Sip.

The waiter brought my order. I managed to get most of the soup down, and I was working on the tea, watching the door, when Kam Fong blew in.

He took half a dozen steps toward the rear, saw me, did an almost comic double take, and reversed direction like a soldier doing an about-face on a parade ground. I got to him just as he was reaching for the doorknob. I caught hold of his arm and wedged him against the door with the right side of my body.

"You're not going anywhere, Fong," I said in an undertone. "We've got things to talk about."

His eyes slid away from my face, rolled in a furtive glance over my shoulder. "Not here. Not talking here."

"Where, then?"

It took him a couple of seconds to think of a place. "Cultural Center. You know it?"

"I know it."

"Fifteen minutes. You come there, yes?"

He made a move for the doorknob again, but I held onto him. "If you don't show up, Fong, I'll come looking for you."

He bobbed his head up and down. I let him go, and he was through the door and away in two seconds. When I turned around one of the waiters and two or three patrons were looking at me; but their faces showed nothing more than curiosity. As soon as I returned to my table, they went back to minding their own business. End of incident.

I finished the rest of my tea, paid the bill, and made my way back to Portsmouth Square. On the east side of it, above the garage, an elevated pedestrian causeway spanned Kearny Street and led to the Financial District branch of the Holiday Inn; the Chinese Cultural Center was at the end of the causeway, on an upper floor of the hotel building. I crossed over and went inside.

It was a big place, museumlike, with several large sculptures, glass cases displaying other forms of Chinese art, an information counter, and an open shop area dispensing books and jade and ivory craftwork. There weren't many visitors, and I didn't see Fong among the few who were present. I moved toward the back. And there he was, looking nervous and frightened, half-hidden behind a massive stone sculpture of a dragon.

He let me prod him over near one of the windows; there was nobody else in the vicinity. But when he spoke it was in a stagey whisper, like a character in a bad play. "Why you come to Mandarin again?"

"Why not? What's the matter?"

"You know," he said accusingly. "You talking to Lee Chuck. Telling him you know about Mau Yee."

"All right, that was a mistake; I admit it. But I didn't use your name."

"Hui Sip finding out, they eat my pie."

"Does Chuck suspect you?"

"No. Not yet, maybe."

"Then don't worry about it."

"I worry," he said. "Worry plenty. Calling you this morning, but nobody home."

"Why did you call?"

"Warning you, don't come back Chinatown."

"Because Mau Yee is looking for me?"

"Yes."

"I already know that. He tried to blow me away last night, outside my flat. He's not going to get a second chance."

Fong grimaced and muttered something in Chinese.

I said, "Is Jimmy Quon the only one after me? Or is it all of Hui Sip?"

"Not knowing. Maybe just Mau Yee."

"What does he look like?"

"Mau Yee? You not seeing him last night?"

"Not up close. Describe him."

"Big," Fong said.

"How big?"

"Like you. Same size."

"What about his features?"

"Pretty. Woman face."

"What else?"

"Cat eyes. Yellow. Look funny."

"Funny how?"

"Only stare, not blinking. *Ah pin yin* eyes."

"What's *ah pin yin?*"

"Opium," he said.

"You mean Quon uses opium?"

"No. Other dope, yes; cocaine, pills. But eyes like *ah pin yin* eater."

"How does he wear his hair?"

"Long. Like woman."

"What about his clothes? Anything distinctive?"

"Western clothes. Leather jacket, all time—brown, with belt. To hide his puppy."

"Uh-huh. Now—"

I paused because a Caucasian woman had wandered back where we were. She gave us a disinterested glance, peered at the dragon sculpture, and wandered away again. When I looked back at Fong he had a small plastic vial in his hand and was popping one of the pills it contained. He had a squirmy look about him, as if he needed to go to the toilet.

Fear does that to some people—swells the bladder, builds up an urge to urinate.

"I go now?" he said. "Somebody belong Hui Sip maybe see us—"

"In here? The. Hui Sip isn't interested in Chinese culture."

"Please. Knowing nothing else about Mau Yee."

"There's still Lee Chuck," I said.

"Already telling you about Lee Chuck—"

"I want more information. Does he allow Caucasians in his gambling parlor?"

"Caucasians?"

"You heard me. High-rolling whites. The poker game, for instance."

He shook his head. "Never asking him. Never gambling there."

"But it is possible? There's no tong rule against Caucasian players?"

"No," Fong said. "Lee Chuck not like *fan quai*, but . . . maybe. If man is known."

"How do you mean 'known'? Connected with Hui Sip somehow?"

"Yes. Or friend of somebody playing all time."

"Does the name Carl Emerson mean anything to you?"

"No."

"You sure you've never heard it before?"

Another head shake. There was blank puzzlement in his eyes; I didn't think he was lying.

"How about the name Philip Bexley?"

"No."

"Orin Tedescu?"

"No."

"Mid-Pacific Electronics?"

"No. What's that?"

"A computer outfit, offices down on Pine Street. Emerson and Bexley and Tedescu are joint partners."

Still another head shake. And the same blank puzzlement.

I leaned toward him, so that my face was just a few inches from his. He started to back up, thought better of it, and stayed where he was; I could smell the sweet-sour odor of his breath, the raw effluvium of his fear.

"Here's what I want you to do," I said. "Check around, find out if any of those three names means anything in Chinatown. Particularly Emerson. You understand?"

"Yes." Then, plaintively, "But you not coming here again? We meet someplace else next time, yes?"

"If you cooperate. If you stay where I can find you when I want you. I'll call your apartment at seven tonight; you be there, whether or not you find out anything."

"Yes. Okay."

"You just hang in there, Fong," I said. "Nothing's going to happen to you or me. The only people who'll get hurt from now on are Jimmy Quon and the man who hired him."

He nodded, but his eyes said he didn't believe it; he had his money down on Mau Yee, fatalistically. But that was all right. He would stay on my side because he had got in over his head and it was his only choice. And I had enough determination for both of us.

"Go on, get out of here," I said. "I'll give you five minutes before I leave."

He sidestepped away from me, let me have a look over his shoulder as if he thought I might be crazy, and scurried off between the displays. He was almost running by the time he reached the front entrance.

I picked up my car and drove it over to Potrero and out to S.F. General to keep my appointment with Doctor Abrams. There was no change in Eberhardt's condition; I asked him about that first thing. "His life signs are stable," Abrams said. "That's the only encouraging news I can give you."

He spent an hour examining me, with not a little displeasure. What had I been doing to inflame the wound that way? Why wasn't I taking care of myself? Didn't I understand that complications could still set in: infection, pneumonia? I told him . had been taking care of myself, that I'd tripped and fallen on my shoulder and that was how the stitch got ripped loose. He made disapproving noises. But then he removed the rest of the stitches, rebandaged the shoulder, and let me go on my way.

It was a quarter of four when I got to my flat. I circled the block a couple of times, looking at the parked cars and the pedestrians; there was no one around who answered Mau Yee's description. When I let myself into the building I had the .38 in my hand, hidden inside my overcoat pocket. Nobody was lurking in the foyer. The apartment was as empty as I had left it, with all the doors and windows still secure.

I brewed some coffee and then called Ben Klein at the Hall of Justice. He had nothing to tell me. He said they were "getting close to a breakthrough," but that was just crap; he sounded frustrated. The police were no closer to Mau Yee than they had been days ago. And they didn't know that I was. If word was out in Chinatown that Jimmy Quon was after me, it had not filtered back to the Department yet; Klein would have said something if they had any inkling of what was going down. The Chinese community was being as closemouthed as usual.

I rang up Ben Chadwick's office in Hollywood. He had nothing to tell me, either. "I've got a request in for information at a couple of places," he said, "but so far, nothing new. Your three boys from Mid-Pacific just aren't known down here."

"Okay. Don't push it. I'm making headway on my own."

"So you *are* working," he said. "You big dumb bastard."

"I've got my reasons."

"What happened to you and your cop friend, is that it?"

"Yeah," I said, "that's it."

"Well, I hope you know what you're doing."

"Me too."

I lay down on the bed for half an hour, to rest and do some thinking. Carl Emerson seemed like the best bet so far to be the man behind Jimmy Quon; but I still could not link him up to Eberhardt. Emerson was a gambler, and gambling was illegal, but the police didn't hassle high rollers, just the parlor operators like Lee Chuck. What could a man like Emerson have done to put Eberhardt on his case? That had to be it, and it had to be something heavily illegal; there was no other possible reason why anyone would try to bribe a police lieutenant. And yet from all I'd learned so far, Emerson was a supposedly reputable businessman.

Well, maybe his ex-wife had some answers for me. She was the only other lead I had at the moment. Except for Emerson himself, and I was not ready yet to confront him.

I got up a little before five, bundled into my overcoat, and went downstairs. I checked the street again before I left the building; still no sign of Quon. And there was nobody on my tail when I drove over to Vallejo Street.

There were no parking spaces near 2860; I had to leave my car three blocks away in a bus zone. This time when I climbed up onto the porch and rang the bell next to Jeanne Emerson's name, the speaker box crackled after ten seconds and a woman's voice said, "Yes, who is it?"

"Mrs. Emerson?"

"Jeanne Emerson, yes?"

"My name is Lloyd Rable," I said. "I'm an investigator

for North Coast Insurance. I'd like to talk to you about your ex-husband, if I may."

Silence for a couple of seconds. Then, "What about him?"

"Mr. Emerson has applied for a large policy with my company. I'm making a standard procedure check into his background."

"You're investigating him?"

"Yes, that's right—a routine investigation. I thought you might be willing to give me a few minutes of your time."

"I'd be happy to. Just a second."

The front door lock began to buzz; I went over and pushed inside. A lobby elevator took me up to the fourth floor. I found 4B, down to the left, and knocked on the door, and it opened on a chain and a woman peered out.

I blinked at her, startled. "Mrs. Emerson?"

"*Ms.* Emerson, if you don't mind," she said.

I gawked a little; I couldn't help it. She was not what I had expected—and yet she was already more than I'd hoped for.

Jeanne Emerson was Chinese.

FOURTEEN

SHE TOOK THE BUSINESS CARD I handed her through the opening, gave it a cursory glance, and then closed the door long enough to remove the chain. "Come in, please."

I went in. She was about thirty, slender, finely boned, with glossy black hair parted in the middle and hanging curtainlike down the small of her back. Her face was a perfect oval, each feature symmetrical; the eyes dominated —olive-black, expressive, slanted only just a little. The only things that kept her from being beautiful were a tracery of lines around the eyes and a bitter curve to her mouth.

When she had the door closed she led me out of a narrow foyer into a Victorian-style living room: heavy old furniture, a couple of Tiffany lamps that may or may not have been genuine, a small Queen Anne fireplace with a marble mantelpiece. The walls were covered with blown-up photographs, most black-and-white, the rest sepia-toned; all of them were contemporary cityscapes, but they had an old-fashioned, almost brooding quality that somehow managed not to be oppressive in that dark room. In one corner, a stereo unit tucked into a cabinet played softly, something classical, with lots of stringed instruments. There was nothing Oriental in the room except her. Even the faces in the photographs were all either black or white.

She indicated a Victorian chaise and I sat down on it. She said, "Would you care for something to drink?"

"Thanks, no."

"Well, I think I'll have a Scotch. I just got home a few minutes ago and it's been a long day."

She went to a sideboard, opened it, took out a bottle and a glass, and poured herself a healthy slug, no ice, no mix. When she came back with it to where I was she caught me looking at the photographs. One in particular—a study of the De Young Museum, clouds piled up the background, people on the steps, that was both sensitive and oddly haunting.

"Do you like them?" she asked. "The photographs?"

"Yes. They're quite good."

"My work," she said with some pride. "I'm a free-lance photojournalist."

"Ah."

"Most of them have appeared in magazines. *New West*, *San Francisco Magazine*, a few others."

"You must be very successful."

She moved one shoulder in a small delicate shrug. "I make a living," she said, and arranged herself on a ladder-back chair with a tufted seat the color of burgundy wine. She was wearing a white blouse and a long black skirt; the skirt made rustling noises when she crossed her legs. She took a sip of her drink and watched me over the rim of the glass, waiting.

I said, "Some of the questions I have to ask are personal. I hope you don't mind."

"Not at all. You said Carl has applied for a large policy with your company?"

"Yes. A life policy. Also a substantial policy on his home in Burlingame."

"I'm sure he can afford it. I understand his company is flourishing these days."

I nodded. "He seems to be solvent, at least as far as Mid-Pacific Electronics is concerned. But I've learned that he has a penchant for gambling."

She smiled faintly, but it didn't reach her eyes; they were

steady, dark with some sort of contained emotion. "That's true," she said. "Gambling is his second favorite pastime."

"His second favorite, did you say?"

"His favorite is women." She said it matter-of-factly. Nothing changed in her expression, except that the curve of her mouth got even more bitter. "But you were asking me about his gambling. You want to know if he loses heavily, I suppose?"

"Yes."

"Not very often, no. He's very good at it."

"Even professional gamblers suffer losses from time to time," I said. "Would you know if he's had any major setbacks in the past few months?"

"No. I haven't seen Carl in close to three years, and we don't communicate."

"You've been divorced four years, is that right?"

"Yes. Four years."

"I understand his favorite game is poker. When you were married did he have a regular place he liked to play? Here in the city, I mean. I know he goes to Las Vegas several times a year."

"Not that I can remember. Carl and I didn't communicate very well then, either."

"Did he ever gamble in Chinatown?"

She took another sip of her Scotch, studying me. "Why do you ask that? Because I'm Chinese?"

"Well . . . yes."

"Are you surprised that he was married to a Chinese woman? You seemed startled when you saw me."

"I guess I was. The issue hadn't come up before."

"If you knew Carl, you wouldn't be surprised."

"Why is that?"

"He has a passion for the Chinese. My people, their way of life—all things Chinese."

So that's it, I thought. The case against Carl Emerson was solidifying, beginning to take shape. He was the man

I wanted; I could feel it now, heavy and growing, like a tumor.

I said, "Does he have many friends in the Chinese community?"

"He has acquaintances. Carl has never had any friends."

"Did he spend much time in Chinatown while you were married?"

"Yes. We lived in Menlo Park—I met him while I was an undergraduate at Stanford—but we used to come into the city two or three times a week for dinner."

"Did he ever indicate to you that he gambled in Chinatown?"

"Yes. He mentioned it."

"Any place in particular?"

"None that he spoke of."

"Does the name Lee Chuck mean anything to you?"

She considered it. "I'm afraid not."

"Hui Sip?"

"A tong," she said. "Not a very benevolent one. What does Hui Sip have to do with Carl's application for insurance?"

Back off a little, I thought. You're making her suspicious. I said, "These are names that came up during the course of my investigation. I've been led to believe that Hui Sip controls gambling in Chinatown; naturally, if Mr. Emerson is involved with them we would consider him a less than satisfactory insurance risk."

"I see."

"Do you know if he's ever had any dealings with Hui Sip?"

"No. But it wouldn't surprise me."

"Why not?"

"They control gambling, just as you said; they also control prostitution. Carl is a gambler and a fornicator and a Chinaphile. No, it wouldn't surprise me."

I frowned. "Do you mean he prefers Chinese women?"

"Exclusively. And obsessively. I doubt if he's ever been to bed with a Caucasian woman."

"But he doesn't consort with prostitutes, does he?"

"Oh yes. Prostitutes, too."

"I don't understand. Why would he do that?"

"He can't get enough of Chinese women," she said. "I wasn't enough for him; the women he meets in social situations and has affairs with aren't enough. Besides, Carl's sexual preferences are . . . exotic."

Her voice was still matter-of-fact; if she felt any embarrassment at making such candid admissions to a stranger, she did not show it any way. I watched her finish her drink and set the glass on a glass-topped table. Things kept stirring around in the back of my mind, like shadows coalescing into recognizable forms. Things Eberhardt had said to me that Sunday afternoon, things I'd been told by others.

I asked her, "Do you know for a fact that he's been with prostitutes?"

"Yes. A friend of mine saw him with one in a Grant Avenue bar one night."

"This was while you were married?"

She nodded. "He admitted it when I confronted him."

"Is that what brought about the divorce?"

"It was the direct cause of my leaving him, yes. I'd suspected for some time before that he was seeing other women."

"Was he upset when you left him?"

"Very. He didn't want to let me go; he never likes to part with any of his possessions. He slapped me around, called me names, threatened me."

"What did you do then?"

"Moved out anyway and came back to the city to live with my sister."

"Did he make any more trouble for you?"

"He tried," she said. "I finally had to get a judge to issue a restraining order against him."

"And he left you alone after that?"

"Yes. Image is important to him; I suppose he was afraid word would get around and harm his business activities."

I was thinking that Emerson was a damned unpleasant son of a bitch, and I said so, but in more polite terms.

"Oh, he can be charming when he wants to be," she said. "He takes in a lot of people with his charm; he fooled me completely at first. It's only when you get to know him that he shows his true colors."

"Had he hit you before the time you left him?"

"No. I can put up with a lot from a man—Chinese women are taught obedience to men from birth—but not that."

"Then normally he's not a violent man?"

"Most of the time he keeps himself under control. But he has a vile temper. There's a lot of violence in Carl, just under the surface."

"What sets him off?"

"Not getting his way. He's an egotist and a borderline sociopath; as far as he's concerned, the universe revolves around Carl Emerson, and everybody else is there for his own personal amusement."

"Has he ever hurt anyone else? Physically, I mean."

"Not that I'm aware of," she said. "He's hurt any number of people, but in more subtle ways."

"Would that number include his business partners?"

"Yes."

"In what way? Neither of them seems to care much for him."

"I'm sure they hate him. He's used them, used their talents; without them, there wouldn't be any Mid-Pacific Electronics."

"But I thought he designed the component Mid-Pacific manufactures."

"No. The original design was Orin Tedescu's. Carl made certain refinements, patented the component in his name; that was his only contribution other than arranging for the financing so they could get started."

"Why did Tedescu go along with that?"

"Carl talked him into it. Orin has no business sense; Carl convinced him their chances of success were greater with his name on the patent, because of his contacts and cachet in the industry."

"What about Bexley?"

"The same thing, more or less. Phil does have a business sense—he's a marketing genius—but he's also insecure. A follower, not a leader. By the time he and Orin realized what Carl had done to them, it was too late; the partnership agreement they'd signed giving Carl controlling interest was ironclad. Carl saw to that."

"So Tedescu and Bexley do most of the work," I said, "and Emerson reaps most of the profits."

"Essentially, yes. About all he does, I'm sure, is give orders, entertain customers, and act as a general supervisor."

"No wonder they're so bitter."

"No wonder we all are," she said.

"Do you hate him, Ms. Emerson?"

"With a passion. That's obvious, isn't it?"

"Then why did you keep his name?"

The delicate shrug again. "When I divorced him I had a line of credit as Jeanne Emerson; it would have presented too many problems to start over again as Jeanne Ng. And it's easier for a Chinese woman to get by professionally if she has a Caucasian name. There's still a lot of prejudice in this world, you know."

"Yes," I said, "I know."

"His name is one of the few useful things I got out of the marriage. I agreed to a very small settlement to avoid any more trouble with him; he would have taken me to court if I hadn't, and I wasn't in any frame of mind for that. I just wanted out."

I thought I understood now why she lived here as she

did, with no Oriental trappings of any kind. She had known too much unhappiness with Emerson, lived too long in the midst of an obsession; it was a kind of backlash effect that had led her to adopt a wholly Westernized life-style. There was no self-delusion in it, no rejection of her heritage; it was evident that she was still proud to *be* Chinese. The trappings themselves were all that she had rejected—her way of burying the past, moving ahead with a new life.

I let a few seconds of silence go by. Then I said, "Well, I think that's about all the information I need. You've been very helpful, Ms. Emerson."

"My pleasure, believe me."

When I got to my feet I felt a small cut of pain in my shoulder; it made me wince. I adjusted the sling a little, and the pain went away.

She said from her chair, "Is your arm bothering you?"

"No, it's okay."

"Gunshot wounds must be very painful," she said.

I was just starting to move away from the chaise; the words stopped me, brought me around. I gawked at her the way I had out in the hallway.

"Oh, yes," she said in the same matter-of-fact voice, "I know who you really are. I recognized you right away. The photograph in the papers wasn't a very good likeness, but photography is my profession. So is journalism, and you've been a major news topic in recent days."

I sat down again, slowly. "Why did you keep up the pretense?"

"I wanted to find out why you'd come. And why you're so interested in Carl. It seemed easier to follow your lead."

"And now? What do you think?"

"I think Carl is involved in the shooting somehow. Or you believe he might be. That's it, isn't it? I can't imagine any other reason why you'd be investigating him, asking questions about his Chinese connections."

I stayed silent.

"If you're worried about me telling him or anyone else," she said, "you needn't be. I wouldn't do that."

"No? You're a journalist."

"Not that kind. Why do you suppose I was so open with you about Carl?"

"Why were you?"

"Because if he *is* mixed up in the shooting, I'd like nothing better than to see him caught and put away. I don't consider myself a vindictive person, but the idea excites me. After all I've told you, I'm sure you can understand that."

"I guess I can," I said. "But I don't know that he is involved."

"But you do believe he is?"

I hesitated. "Maybe."

"In what way?"

"I'd rather not say. It's only supposition at this point."

"Are the police investigating him, too?"

"No. I don't think so."

"Okay, I won't press you anymore. I'm sure you know what you're doing. You're a good detective; you've proven that. The police gave you a raw deal when they suspended your license and I don't blame you for working independently of them. Just tell me this: Do you think it'll be long before you know for certain if Carl is involved?"

"No," I said, "it won't be long."

"Good. If there's anything else I can do, just let me know."

I nodded. "There is one other thing. I've never seen Emerson and I don't know what he looks like. A description would help."

"I can do better than that," she said. "I can show you a photograph of him. I kept one, for my portfolio. Not because of any sentimental reason; only because I took it and it's rather good."

She got up and left the room for a couple of minutes.

When she came back she handed me an 8 × 10 black-and-white glossy. It was a head-and-shoulders portrait of a tall blond man with aristocratic features, a heavy underlip, and eyes that were both shrewd and petulant. He was handsome, and he was smiling, but there were shadows on his face, an unmistakable sense of weakness and cruelty in his expression. I wondered if it had been a conscious effort on her part to capture his negative aspects. If so, she had succeeded—and maybe that was another reason why she'd kept the photograph.

"You can borrow it if you like," she said. "But I would like it back."

"No, that won't be necessary. I'll remember him. He's got the kind of face you don't forget."

"Yes," she said. "No matter how hard you might want to try."

She went with me to the foyer, and when she opened the door she gave me her hand. Her eyes seemed to linger on my face. "I'd like to see you again when this is finished. And not just because of Carl."

"Why?"

"You're an interesting man. And you're also a victim of the system. I think I'd like to do a piece on you for one of the magazines."

"Are you serious?"

"Very serious. Would you be agreeable?"

"I don't know. I'd have to think it over."

"Do that. Meanwhile, good luck."

"Thanks."

"And good hunting," she said.

Out in the hallway, I stood looking at the door for a few seconds after she closed it. I had never met a woman quite like Ms. Jeanne Emerson before, and she'd left me feeling a little nonplussed. She was some lady.

But I felt more grim than anything else. If I could believe everything she'd told me, and I thought I could, I had a stronger case than ever against Carl Emerson. I also had a pretty good hunch as to what lay behind this whole thing —the reason why he had bribed or tried to bribe Eberhardt, the reason why he'd hired Jimmy Quon to blow Eb away. And I did not like it worth a damn.

The hunch was a dead hooker named Polly Soon.

FIFTEEN

ON THE WAY OVER to North Beach, I kept thinking about Emerson's probable motives. My hunch was based on three things. First, the revelation that he was a Chinaphile, had a penchant for Chinese prostitutes, and owned a violent temper. Second, the fact that Polly Soon had fallen to her death from a fifth-floor walkway at the Ping Yuen housing project a couple of weeks ago; both Ben Klein and Richard Loo had told me it was a case Eberhardt had been working on. And third, bits and pieces of what Eberhardt had said to me before Jimmy Quon showed up with his .357 Magnum that Sunday afternoon:

"I hate my goddamn job sometimes. It's a hell of a thing being a cop, you know that?"

"Somebody's got to do it. And you're one of the best."

"Am I? I don't know about that."

And:

"You don't know what I'm liable to do; neither do I."

And:

"Whores are better off dead anyway. Who cares about a damned whore?"

Put all of those things together, juggle them with a few other facts I had learned about Carl Emerson, and they added up this way:

Emerson picks up Polly Soon at a Chinatown bar—either that, or they've had an ongoing relationship—and takes her back to the project. Something happens after they arrive, maybe an argument of some kind, and Emerson loses his temper. Polly Soon tries to get away; Emerson goes after her, out onto the walkway that runs across the front of the building. There's a scuffle, and she either falls accidentally or Emerson pushes her over the railing. Then he manages to get away without being identified by any of her neighbors.

When the initial police investigation doesn't turn him up he thinks he's got away clean. But Eberhardt is a tenacious cop; somehow he gets on to Emerson, with enough proof of Emerson's guilt to confront him. Emerson's only out is to offer a bribe lucrative enough to keep Eberhardt from arresting him and filing an official report. Only something goes wrong with the scheme; maybe Eberhardt has second thoughts, maybe Emerson decides the stock-transfer payoff wasn't such a good idea after all because it leaves him vulnerable. In any case, he opts to take the big plunge into premeditated homicide and hires Jimmy Quon. Emerson knows his way around Chinatown, has probably done some gambling at Lee Chuck's; it wouldn't have been difficult for him to find out which Hui Sip body-washer was willing to waste a cop for the right price. Lee Chuck himself might have acted as the go-between; that would explain how he knew it was Quon who pulled the trigger, and why.

A nice, tight little scenario. And I hated it because it meant Eberhardt had not only taken a bribe but done it to cover up a homicide.

The thought gave me a sick, ulcerous feeling in my stomach. You go through life believing in certain things, certain people; they're central to your outlook, your whole philosophy of right and wrong, good and bad; they're what you hang on to when the going gets tough. Take them away, one by one, and what did you have left? Nothing, an existence without meaning. That was what was happening to me. Six weeks of erosion, of psychic crumbling, that had reduced my little corner of the world to a pile of rubble. All

I could do was to poke around in the ruins, try to rebuild this or that place of meaning so I could go on living there. Only with most of them it seemed to be too late; they kept on crumbling when I touched them, disintegrating into handfuls of dust.

There was not much left now. A few bricks of justice, maybe; I still had those. Emerson was going to pay for what he'd done. So was Jimmy Quon. And so was Eberhardt, if it came to that.

I found a place to park near the Central Station precinct house on Vallejo. Over near Broadway, there was a neighborhood bar called Luigi's; I went in there and back to a public telephone near the restrooms. It was just seven o'clock when I dialed Kam Fong's number. I had told him to be there at seven, and he was; he answered on the second ring.

"What did you find out?" I asked him.

"Only man name Emerson known here," he said. "Other two, no."

"How is Emerson known? As a gambler?"

"Yes."

"Does he frequent Lee Chuck's parlor?"

"Sometimes."

"Did you get that from Chuck?"

"No. Not talking to him."

"What about the local whores?"

"Please? Not understand."

"Emerson likes them too, doesn't he? Chinese whores?"

"Nobody talking about that."

"Someone talked to me about it. Did you know Polly Soon?"

Silence.

"Come on, Fong. Polly Soon—did you know her?"

"I . . . yes."

"How well?"

"Not well. Nobody know whore well."

"Did she take on Caucasian tricks?"

"Yes, maybe."

"How did she die? You hear anything about that?"

"No."

"Did Lieutenant Eberhardt ask you about her?"

"He asking, but I having no answer."

"Who else did he talk to?"

"Don't know. You think Polly Soon's death . . . ?"

"That's just what I think. Did she have any close friends? Another prostitute? One of her neighbors?"

Silence.

"I'm waiting, Fong," I said.

"Maybe . . . woman name Ming Toy."

"Also a hooker?"

"Yes."

"Where does she live? In the Ping Yuen project?"

"Yes."

"Alone?"

"Yes."

"Have you been to her apartment?"

"No. Not visiting whores."

"I'll bet," I said. "What floor does she live on?"

"Fifth floor."

"What apartment?"

"Near Polly Soon. Next door."

"Did you tell the lieutenant about Ming Toy?"

"Yes."

"When? Right after Polly Soon was killed?"

"No. Later. He asking me find out who Polly Soon's friend."

"How much later? A few days before the shooting, maybe?"

"I think yes."

"Do you know if he talked to her?"

"No, not knowing."

"All right. Does Ming Toy work the bars too?"

"Bars, yes."

"Any one in particular?"

"Pink Dragon Bar."

"Where's that?"

"Broadway."

"Near Grant?"

"Yes."

"What does she look like? Describe her."

"Very small. Long pigtail."

"How old?"

"Over thirty. But she look young, like teenager. People here . . . they calling her China Doll."

Yeah, I thought, China Doll. I said, "Is there anybody else who was close to Polly Soon? Any other names you gave to the lieutenant?"

"No. No one else."

"Okay, Fong. You stick around there in case I need to talk to you again. Don't go out anywhere tonight."

He muttered something in Chinese. Then he said, with a kind of nervous resignation, "You call any time, I stay here."

"Good enough."

I cradled the receiver and went back out to the street. Dusk was just starting to spread over the city. On Broadway and along Columbus, the garish neon signs advertising the North Beach topless and bottomless joints were already ablaze, softened and given a misty sheen by the fog. There was more fog now than there had been earlier—a thickening mist wind-blown in from the sea, chill and wet and sinuous, eerie in its movements and distortions. Such heavy fog this early in the evening usually meant a London-style pea-souper later on. It was going to be some night.

I pulled the collar of my overcoat tight around my throat, walked down to the intersection of Broadway and Columbus, and crossed over into Chinatown.

The Ping Yuen housing project took up most of the block of Pacific Avenue between Grant and Stockton, a couple of blocks from the Pink Dragon Bar where the China Doll plied her trade. It was one long, tall structure, divided into wings and oddly designed so that it resembled a bastardized architectural hybrid of Chinese pagoda–style and Western motel–style. It was painted a faded pastel green, with rust-red pillars and support posts that had Chinese characters etched into them in black. Set behind an iron-spear fence, the building had a forlorn, decaying look in the fog and approaching darkness.

I pushed through the main entrance gate, under a pagoda arch bearing four statues of stylized Oriental lions. Inside, there was a narrow pebbled-concrete courtyard with some benches and a few shrubs and spindly trees. It would be somewhere in there, on that hard concrete, that Polly Soon had died. A scattering of lights on poles illuminated the area, and there were more lights glowing hazily on the upper walkways and in the windows of the blocky wings between them.

Nobody was hanging around in the courtyard, or at least nobody I could see. I crossed it to a bank of mailboxes, only a few of which bore names; none of the names was Ming Toy's. I got into a creaking elevator festooned with spray-painted initials and let it carry me up to the fifth floor. As soon as I stepped out I was on the open walkway of the lower wing. The wind blew cold up there; that, and the fact that I was prone to vertigo in high, open places like this, forced me in close to the building wall. The outer portion of the walkway was a thin waist-high wall, with no railing on top of it. It would be easy enough for somebody to fall over it, either by accident or design.

It took me ten minutes and three brief interviews with fifth-floor residents to find out that Ming Toy occupied Apartment 515, in the middle wing. When I got to the door marked with those numerals I rapped on it with my knuckles; there wasn't any doorbell. Silence from inside. I rapped again, louder, but that did not get me any response, either.

Nobody home.

I tried the knob. Locked. I thought about trying to slip the latch with one of my credit cards—it was that kind of lock—but I didn't do it. If I was going to learn anything from Ming Toy, it would probably be face to face. Which made finding her my first priority. I could always come back here later on if nothing else worked out.

The Pink Dragon Bar was set back from the street under an arched portico, halfway between Grant and Stockton. The front wall and door were painted black, with a stylized pink dragon curled around the door, breathing bright red flame toward the pavement. But I was tired of looking at dragons; the hell with dragons and the hell with dragonfire. I shoved open the door and went inside.

Dark, with pinkish lights over the bar, pink lanterns on a handful of tables and six booths arranged around a rectangular dance floor. Noisy: a jukebox was playing rock music at full volume. The place was only about a third filled, with most of the customers grouped along the bar. Nearly all of them were Caucasian males. The only Chinese women in evidence were a couple of waitresses in pink miniskirts, and an overweight hooker rubbing herself against a potential john in one of the booths.

I edged up to the bar, down at the end where nobody was sitting. The bartender was a youngish guy with a Fu Manchu mustache; he wore a pink jacket with a dragon embroidered over the pocket. When he got around to me I leaned forward and said, "I'm looking for the China Doll."

He'd heard that before; one corner of his mouth lifted in a wise smile. Fine. He thought I was just another john and that was what I wanted him to think.

"Not here," he said.

"She be in later?"

"Maybe. It depends."

"She's a regular, though, isn't she?"

"She drops in most nights."

"What time, if she's coming?"

"Around nine. Something to drink while you wait?"

I thought it over. I could hang around here or I could go out hunting for Ming Toy. But there were a lot of flesh spots in Chinatown and in North Beach; I could wander around all night without finding her. And the less I exposed myself to people on Jimmy Quon's turf, the better off I would be. The smart thing to do was to stay put for an hour or two.

I said, "Bottle of Schlitz. I'll take it in a booth."

The booth I claimed was positioned so that you could see the front door from inside it. One of the waitresses brought the beer, gave me a sloe-eyed look, took my money, and went away again. I poured beer and sat nursing it, not thinking about anything, letting the rock music from the juke fill up my head.

And I waited.

Sixteen

The China Doll showed up at twenty minutes past nine.

I was working on my second beer, fighting off impatience, when I saw her come in. Even in the dim pinkish light, I recognized her immediately: tiny, young-looking, wearing a Chinese dress slit to the thigh, the long pigtails Kam Fong had mentioned pulled forward so that they hung over her breasts. The place was crowded now, and she came forward in slow, dainty movements, looking at the faces of the men she passed, like a predator sizing up her prey.

I was out of the booth and moving toward her before she got to the end of the bar. One of the men turned on his stool and said something to her; she stopped to answer him. But when I reached her, coming up close, she turned her head and tilted it back to peer up at me.

She was no more than five feet tall; the top of her head was on a level with my chest. Too much makeup and powder gave her face a whitish cast, and her mouth looked painted on. China Doll, all right. Life-sized doll, soft and cuddly, that would do things the toy manufacturers never dreamed of.

I said, "Ming Toy?"

"Yes?" Sibilant piping voice, as if it were coming out of a box implanted in her throat.

"I've got a twenty-dollar bill in my wallet. It's yours if you sit down and have a drink with me."

Her gaze slid down my body like a caress, flicked up again to my face; the eyes, under long artificial lashes, were old and wise and black as midnight. The point of her tongue came out and made her painted lips glisten.

The guy at the bar nudged me with one hand. I looked at him, and he said, "Hey, buddy, I saw her first." I kept on looking at him, not saying anything, until he started to fidget. Then I said, "Drink your drink—buddy," and he mumbled something and swiveled away from me with his shoulders hunched.

When I looked at Ming Toy again her tongue was still showing between her teeth, like a cat's. "Twenty dollars," I said. "For a drink and some conversation. That's all."

"I would be honored."

Yeah, I thought. I took her arm and steered her back to the booth, and we sat down. She folded her hands on the table, watching me as I got the twenty out of my wallet. But I didn't give it to her, not yet; I folded it in half and put it under my beer glass. "Talk first," I said. "All right?"

"Yes."

The waitress came over, took the China Doll's order for a daiquiri, and went away again. The damned jukebox began to give out with another loud song, all hammering drums and lyrics that sounded like gibberish. I leaned closer to Ming Toy so that my face was only a few inches from hers. The tongue came out again, like an invitation this time; but her eyes were hooded and wary, watching.

I told her my name, my right name. The artificial lashes fluttered once, but that was all; nothing changed in her expression. "You know who I am?" I asked her.

"No," she said. "We have met before?"

"We haven't met. But we both know some people."

"Yes?"

"Yes. A cop named Eberhardt, for one."

Still no change in her expression. But after a few seconds she nodded and said, "So," in a different voice, without the whisper of sex in it.

"You know me now?" I said.

"Yes. I think so."

"Good. What do you know?"

"You the man who was shot. You and the policeman."

"What else?"

"Nothing else."

"Then I'll tell you," I said. "The man who shot Eberhardt and me is a Chinese named Jimmy Quon. You know who he is, don't you?"

Her hands moved together on the table; she was nervous now, and there was fear peeking out at the edges of the whore's mask. "Everyone know Mau Yee," she said. "But why you come to me? I have nothing to do with him."

"It's not Mau Yee I'm interested in right now. It's the man who hired him, a white man named Carl Emerson."

She looked away from me, biting her lip. The waitress came back just then, and when she set the daiquiri down Ming Toy caught it up immediately and took an unladylike bite out of it. I got rid of the waitress with some money and bent toward the China Doll again.

I said, "You've had dealings with Emerson before," making it a statement instead of a question.

"I . . . yes."

"One of your customers?"

"Yes."

"One of Polly Soon's customers?"

"I don't . . . why you ask about Polly Soon?"

"You were a friend of hers, weren't you?"

A convulsive nod. And another bite out of the daiquiri, this time with both hands wrapped around the glass.

"How did she die, Ming Toy?"

"She fell. . . . It was an accident. . . ."

"Was it? How do you know? Were you there when it happened?"

"No," she said, a little too quickly.

"You live on the same floor at the Ping Yuen project. You sure you weren't there that night? You sure you didn't see Polly Soon fall?"

"No!"

"Did Carl Emerson push her off that walkway?"

"I don't know. . . ."

"But he was with her that night?"

"I didn't see them. I wasn't there."

"Is that what you told Lieutenant Eberhardt?"

"Yes, I . . ." She blinked. "You know he spoke to me?"

"I do now. What else did you tell him?"

"Nothing. I know nothing about Polly's death."

"You must have told him something, given him some kind of lead. Did you mention Emerson's name?"

"No."

"Did he mention it?"

"No."

"Another name, then? Somebody else that he went to see?"

She hesitated. Then she said, "Anna Chu."

"Who's Anna Chu?"

"Old woman who lives in the project. She minds the business of others."

"You think maybe she saw something that night?"

"Maybe yes."

"Do you know if the lieutenant talked to her?"

"No. Anna Chu and I don't speak; she don't like me."

"What's her apartment number?"

"Five-eleven. But she won't be there now."

"Why not?"

"She . . . stay late on Tuesday nights. At the temple."

"What temple?"

"The temple of Tien Hou. She's one of the caretakers."

I had heard of the Tien Hou Temple; it was one of Chinatown's fixtures, and there had been a feature article on it in the Sunday papers some time back. Tien Hou was a Chinese goddess, queen of heaven and the sea, protector of sailors, traveling actors, and prostitutes. Yeah, I thought, prostitutes. Tien Hou must have been looking the other way the night Polly Soon died.

I said, "It's on Waverly Place, isn't it?"

"Yes."

"And Anna Chu will be there now?"

"Until midnight. Every Tuesday."

I took the twenty out from under my glass, held it up in front of her. She made a grab for it. I let her get her fingers on the bill, but I hung onto it. "Is there anything else you told the lieutenant? Any other name you gave him?"

"No."

"You'd better be sure," I said. "If I find out different, I'll be back for another talk. You understand?"

"I have told you everything."

I let go of the twenty. She stuffed it inside the bead purse she was carrying, slid out of the booth in hurried movements; she wasn't looking at me anymore. I got out right after her, saw her move toward the rear of the room, saw a guy at one of the tables paw at her as she passed and Ming Toy swat his hand away. Then she was gone and so was I, on my way to find Anna Chu.

The two-block length of Waverly Place was shrouded in fog so dense you could not see more than fifty yards in either direction. What few pedestrians there were appeared and disappeared like wraiths; street lamps and neon signs seemed to hang suspended in midair, and the buildings— joss houses, darkened shops, restaurants, the headquarters of several tongs and fraternal organizations—had an insubstantial, two-dimensional look, as if they were adrift in the swirling grayness. It was the kind of night that works on your imagination, gives you the feeling that you're surrounded by menace.

The building that housed the Tien Hou Temple was in the block between Clay and Washington. Narrow, four-storied, with ornate balconies on the upper two floors, its pagoda cornices hidden in the mist. The lower floors were dark, but I could make out faint, diffused bars of light coming through shutters beyond the top-floor balcony. A pair of bright yellow signs with red lettering in both English and Chinese, one above the glass entrance door and one attached to it, said that the temple could be found within. The door itself was unlocked.

Inside was a staircase, not very well lighted, and nothing else. On the second-floor landing there was a heavily barred door with some sort of insignia on it that I didn't bother to look at, and on the third floor I passed another door, this one unbarred, marked with Chinese characters. I kept climbing, panting a little with the exertion, and when the stairs made a circular turning I was looking at an iron gate that blocked off access at the top. An old-fashioned doorbell had been installed in the wall near it, and below that was a hand-lettered sign that said Tien Hou was the oldest Chinese temple in America and asked for donations to keep it operating.

I pushed the bell button, but nothing happened inside. I did not even hear it ring; the only sound to hear anywhere in the building was the rasp of my own breathing. Maybe the thing doesn't work, I thought. I put the tips of my fingers against the gate and gave it a tentative push, the way you do, and it swung inward; the gate hadn't been shut far enough to secure the latch. I went in through it, eased it closed behind me.

"Hello? Anna Chu?"

No answer.

I was in a partitioned alcove full of tables and boxes and

folding chairs, a kind of storage area. The temple was on my left; reddish light glowed in there. I could see the closed louvered doors to the balcony, a recessed side altar made of red-painted wood with some sort of statue inside it. The pungent odor of incense was strong in the air, and stronger still when I entered the temple proper.

It was some place. The long side wall facing me was lined with altars, statues, teak tables and other pieces of furniture, nearly all of them in red and gold. A massive scrolled wood carving, covered in gold leaf, stretched the width of the room overhead; the rest of the ceiling was taken up with dozens of hanging lanterns in pink and green, red and gold. A long table draped in white cloth and stacked with paper-craft was set along the near wall. At the upper end were a pair of great carved altars, one that took up the entire back wall and another, with a red prayer bench fronting it, set apart in the middle of the floor. Both of these, and the smaller altars on the far side, were arranged with embroidered cloths, bowls of oranges and apples, potted crysan-themums, joss urns, red-hued electric candles, and other things I could not identify.

There was no sign of anybody in the room. I called Anna Chu's name again, still didn't get an answer, and moved ahead toward the main altars. To my left, beyond the white-draped table, was a short ell containing a bench for the storage of incense and a red-painted platform that supported an ancient drum and a heavy iron temple bell. When I got to where I could see the floor next to the platform I came to an abrupt standstill. The hackles went up on my neck; without thinking about it, I yanked the .38 out of my coat pocket and held it upraised in my hand.

Somebody was lying over there, face down, legs and arms outflung. But it wasn't Anna Chu because it wasn't a woman. Alongside the sprawled form was an ornamental altar standard, like a spear or a pikestaff, that had come out of a row of similar standards on the wall behind the altar;

part of the bronze symbol decorating its head was clotted with blood. So was the back of the man's skull—what was left of it. He had to have been struck down with savage force to cause that much damage.

My stomach kicked over a couple of times, pumped the taste of bile into my throat. I went over to him, around next to the temple bell. I was pretty sure I knew who he was even before I did that, but seeing his face gave me an even greater feeling of incredulity. He shouldn't have been here and he shouldn't have been dead, and I could not put the two facts together so that they made any kind of sense. I just kept standing there, confused, smelling the incense and fighting off nausea, staring down at the body in the dim ruby light from the lanterns and the electric candles.

The dead man was Jimmy Quon.

SEVENTEEN

It was at least fifteen seconds before I could make myself move again. Then I set my teeth and knelt beside the body, not looking at his face anymore. His expression was the stuff of nightmares: yellowish eyes open and bulging like a frog's; effeminate mouth twisted into a rictus, shiny with blood, so that it looked as though he was grinning.

He was wearing the brown leather jacket Kam Fong had told me about; I bunched it up away from his waist. There was no sign of the .357 Magnum or of any other weapon. If he always went armed, then whoever had killed him must have taken his puppy. Why?

Why any of this?

I laid the .38 on the floor, got out my handkerchief, and went through the jacket pockets. Pack of cigarettes, half of which were hand-rolled marijuana joints, some matches, and nothing else. Nothing in his Levi's except half a roll of Velamints, a ring of keys, and a wallet. I used the handkerchief to slide the wallet out. Close to a hundred dollars in cash, a driver's license, a couple of cards embossed with Chinese characters that were probably organizational membership cards, and a tattered, palm-sized address book. The book told me nothing; all the entries were in Chinese.

I put the wallet back into his pocket, caught up the .38, and shoved to my feet. The temple had become oppressive —too quiet, too red, heavy with a sense of desecration. And the incense, the faint underlying odor of death, was making me gag. Get out of here, I thought; you can't think in here. And you don't want to be around if anybody else shows up.

There was a walk-space between the two main altars; I detoured through it, thinking of Anna Chu, but the floor back there was empty. Out in the front alcove, I eased open the gate and stood listening. The stairwell and the rest of the building were hushed. I went down slowly, holding the gun pointed downward along my thigh. I did not put it away until I got to the street door at the bottom.

The sidewalk in front was deserted. I turned left, into the eddies of fog; the wet, brackish odor of it chased away the lingering vestiges of the incense. When I got to Washington I found a quiet-looking neighborhood tavern and went in and sat at the bar, away from the knot of other customers. I needed time to think, to make some sense out of Jimmy Quon's murder, before I could decide on my next move.

Who had killed him? Somebody else in Hui Sip, another *boo how doy*? Revenge motive, maybe? Not likely. Convenient coincidence? I did not like that much. All right. It had to be tied into the shooting, and that meant one obvious candidate: the man who had hired Quon in the first place, Carl Emerson.

But why? A falling-out of some kind? That was possible, but why would it have happened in the Tien Hou Temple? It was an unlikely place for a rendezvous. Then why would Emerson go there? Why would Quon go there? Quon might have gone to see Anna Chu, if she *did* know something about Polly Soon's death and if she *had* talked to Eberhardt and if Emerson was afraid she'd talk to somebody else . . . no, that didn't add up. Polly Soon had been dead more than three weeks, the bribe to Eberhardt had taken place two weeks ago; if Emerson had been worried about a witness, he could have used Quon to find out about Anna Chu the same way both Eberhardt and I had, through

Ming Toy, long before this. And maybe Emerson had found out about her, maybe Eberhardt himself had given him her name, and he'd bribed her, too.

Possible. But then I was right back to zero. Why had Quon gone to the temple tonight? Why was Emerson there? Yes, and where was Anna Chu?

Maybe there isn't any Anna Chu, I thought.

The possibility came bubbling up out of my subconscious, and right behind it a whole bunch of other possibilities. I sat still, letting them take shape.

Suppose Ming Toy had lied to me earlier. Suppose *she* was the witness after all—she lived on the same floor as Polly Soon, she could have been home that night—and suppose Emerson had got to her and paid her off to keep her mouth shut. She'd be afraid of him, and even more afraid of Quon. She'd do anything Mau Yee told her to do. Like lying to me. Like giving me a phony name and sending me up to the temple.

A set up.

Sure, it made sense that way. I go to the Pink Dragon and ask for Ming Toy; somebody there, the bartender or the waitress who'd given me the sloe-eyed look, is a friend of the China Doll's and has been alerted to contact her if a big guy with one arm in a sling comes around asking for her. Quon's doing, probably; he'd want to know right away if I started sniffing around Ming Toy. So the friend gets in touch with her, and she gets in touch with Quon, and he tells her to send me to the Tien Hou. He knows I'm on my guard and he wants to throw me off it. What better place for an ambush than a temple, a house of worship?

Only something had screwed up the plan. What? Where did Emerson come into it?

Well, suppose he was with Quon when the call came from the China Doll. Or showed up just afterward, before Quon left for the temple. Okay, but why would he go along? He wouldn't want to be present at the ambush;

that wasn't his style. He wanted me dead, yes, but—

Wait now, I thought. *Does* he want me dead?

If he wasn't aware that I'd talked to Tedescu and Bexley, he might not suspect that I was on to him. All he'd know was that I was on to Jimmy Quon. Quon would have told him that much; but Quon couldn't have told him I'd been asking questions about Emerson because he hadn't known it. I had not used Emerson's name when I confronted Lee Chuck, and it was only after the setup had been arranged tonight that I'd asked Ming Toy about Emerson.

The only people who knew about his connection with the death of Polly Soon, as far as Emerson was concerned, were Eberhardt and Quon and Ming Toy. He'd bought Ming Toy's silence, and there was nothing he could do about Eberhardt. But Quon was another matter. In his eyes, Quon might have seemed much more dangerous to him than I was, particularly after the abortive attempt on my life last night. Suppose Emerson hadn't sanctioned that; suppose he'd been upset about it when Quon told him what had happened, because he was afraid that kind of open warfare would blow the whole thing wide open. If I got Mau Yee before he got me, and Quon survived and talked, Emerson was in the soup.

But if Quon was out of the picture, it would eliminate one major threat and neutralize the one I presented. The way Emerson would see it, I'd have nowhere to go; maybe I'd back off and maybe I'd keep looking, but with Quon dead it wouldn't matter either way. Ming Toy was in his pocket, and he'd just have to hope Eberhardt died without coming out of his coma. There were no other links, no other way for me to tie on to him.

It was panic reasoning, but Emerson had to be panicked by this time. Trying to burn his bridges was something he might have opted for. If that was it, then it was clear enough what had gone down tonight. He'd followed Mau Yee to the temple, made some excuse for showing up, and then used the altar standard to crush Quon's skull when his back was turned. By the time I got there, he was long gone.

Gone where? Would he go after Ming Toy, try to burn that bridge too? He might think the money he'd given her was enough to ensure her silence, he might not; it all depended on how panicked he was, how homicidal. He could be out looking for her. Or he could have gone home to Burlingame. Or, hell, he could be anywhere by now.

So what was my move? I could go looking for Ming Toy myself, but even if I could find her, it would be an exercise in futility if Emerson had decided to leave her alone. No, it was Emerson I had to find, not the China Doll. Two choices, then. One was Burlingame, but I did not want to drive all the way down there, not yet. There was a chance he was still in Chinatown, and if he was, I knew one place he might have gone—to establish an alibi, if for no other reason, in order to keep the Hui Sip from looking his way when they learned Jimmy Quon was dead.

Lee Chuck's gambling parlor.

Ross Alley was deserted, choked with fog, when I came into it off Jackson Street. My shoes made hollow, muffled clicks on the damp pavement; there were no other sounds except for the whisper of cars drifting up the hill behind me, the tinny beat of music from the pair of bars down the way. A neon sign over one of the bars, half hidden, gave the mist a reddish tint, as if it had been stained with blood. Blobs of pale light marked the windows of the second-floor bundle shops, and there were night-lights burning in a couple of the small stores—one of them Lee Chuck's herb shop.

I stepped into the alcove there, peered through the door glass; there was nothing to see. And nothing to see in the second-floor windows along the alley: no sign of a lookout. I leaned over finally and banged on the adjacent door, the one that hung crooked in its frame. Then I got the .38 out and flattened back against the shop door, away from the crooked one. And waited.

Pretty soon the peephole opened; I could hear it and I could see the faint outspill of light just before the guy in there filled the hole with his eye. But he could not see me where I was standing. The light reappeared as he pulled his head back; then the lid came back over the hole and shut it off. The door stayed closed.

I reached out and whacked it again, using the gun this time. The doorman repeated his peephole ritual, and when he still didn't see anything it annoyed him. I heard him mutter something softly in Chinese.

Come on, I thought. Open the goddamn door.

He opened it. The lock scraped, the door edged inward; he poked his head out. I moved over, wedged my shoulder against the door, and crowded into him, through the opening and inside. He made a startled grunting noise, staggered, and caught himself with one hand on the wall. I went right up against him and jammed the gun in his stomach.

"Make a move," I said, "make a sound, I'll put a bullet in you."

He was young, brawny, with a wispy beard and not much chin. He didn't show me any fear, but he didn't move or speak, either. The door was still open; I backed off from him a couple of steps and pushed it shut with my foot. We were in a small foyer, maybe ten feet square, lighted by a low-wattage bulb screwed into a wall socket. Under the light was a chair and a tiny table with some Chinese magazines on it. A flight of steep stairs stood opposite; I couldn't see all the way to the top, but I could hear voices from up there, the steady clicking of coins and tiles and poker chips.

"Upstairs," I said to the doorman. "Move."

He stayed where he was, watching me through eyes narrowed down to slits.

I thumbed the hammer back on the .38. That made up

his mind for him; he shoved away from the wall and went over to the stairs. I lowered the hammer, put the gun with my hand around it into my coat pocket, and then moved up behind him and jabbed the muzzle into the small of his back. We went up crowded together like a couple of old friends.

At the top there was a landing with a blank wall at the end of it; the parlor was on the left, beyond a wide doorway. I prodded the doorman inside. Big room, blue with smoke; floored in linoleum, filled with imitation leather furniture, old-fashioned smoking stands, and maybe a dozen gaming tables. The tables were all covered in white felt and each of them had a silver-shaded lamp hanging low over it. Half were fan-tan layouts with nothing on them but mounds of little brass coins that had square holes in the middle, presided over by housemen with ivory-handled rakes. There were two four-seat Mah-Jongg tables cluttered with dice and green-and-white tiles; the rest were six-sided poker tables. Maybe forty people occupied the room, all men and all but two of them Chinese.

Neither of the Caucasians was Carl Emerson.

Most of the gamblers were grouped around the fan-tan layouts, probably because fan-tan was a simple game and required no particular skill; the houseman used his rake to pull coins two at a time off the pile, and the betting was on whether one or two would remain at the end. The two white guys were playing poker. Both of them gave me cursory glances and then looked back at their cards. The Chinese were more curious; some of them stopped talking and their gazes lingered on me, wary and speculative.

But I did not pay any attention to them. I was looking at the rear of the room, where a glass-fronted cubicle spanned the entire wall. That was the bank, and through the glass I could see Lee Chuck sitting on a high stool behind a counting desk, like an Oriental despot surveying his domain.

He was bent forward in an attitude of concentration, horn-rimmed glasses pushed down on the tip of his nose, writing something in an oversized ledger; he hadn't seen me yet. I nudged the doorman with my shoulder to get him moving again, and we went along the side wall past a couple of the fan-tan layouts, toward the cubicle. We were halfway there when Chuck raised his head. I saw him stiffen, but that was his only reaction; he kept on sitting on his stool, staring out as we approached.

There was a door on the near side of the cubicle, open and guarded by another young, heavyset Chinese, this one in a business suit. He was probably armed; not all of the bulges under the suit jacket were muscles. He was watching us, too, with the same wary speculation as the players.

In an undertone I said to the doorman, "We're going inside. Tell the guard Lee Chuck is expecting me. In English."

He didn't give any indication that he'd heard me. I was pretty tensed up by this time; I did not want to have to use the gun, and I wouldn't use it unless it became a matter of self-preservation, but if the doorman or the guard made trouble, somebody was going to get hurt just the same. I was in a mood to break the place up if that was what it took to get to Chuck.

But there was no trouble. When we reached the cubicle the doorman said what I'd told him to say, and the guard looked me up and down and then glanced in at Chuck for confirmation. Maybe Chuck sensed the potential for violence, or maybe the house was having a big night and he didn't want to disrupt the gaming, or maybe he was just curious; in any case, all he did was nod. The guard stepped aside, and the doorman and I went in through the open doorway.

Lee Chuck got off his stool as I elbowed the door shut. The glass wall was fairly thick; the babble of voices in the parlor receded. The doorman said something in Chinese that sounded like an apology. Chuck didn't look at him; behind the horn-rims his eyes poked at my face like rough stones.

I said, "I've got a gun in my pocket. I can show it to you if you want."

"No. I believe you."

"Good. Just so you understand I'm not playing games."

"What is it you wish here?"

"I'm looking for Carl Emerson," I said.

"Emerson, sir?"

"No more bullshit, Chuck; I'm tired of bullshit. I want Emerson and I'm going to get him. If I have to walk on you to do it, I will."

He let a small silence build. The doorman had gone over to a big black-and-gold safe and was leaning against it, looking sullen. On a table behind the desk, a Persian cat lay sprawled on its side; it seemed to be watching me too.

Chuck said finally, "Why do you want this man Emerson?"

"You know why I want him. But there's another reason, too. When I tell you what it is I think you'll agree to help me find him."

"Yes?"

"Yes. He murdered Jimmy Quon tonight. At the Tien Hou Temple."

Chuck blinked, just once, the first time he had ever blinked in my presence; it was about as much indication of startlement as anyone would ever get out of him. He didn't say anything.

I glanced out through the glass. The heavyset guard was half-turned so that he could watch what was going on in here; some of the gamblers were still rubbernecking. It made me uneasy, being on display like this. The longer I stayed around here, the more chance there was of things stirring up into a skirmish.

"What we're going to do," I said to Chuck, "we're going to walk out of here and go downstairs to the herb shop. There's more privacy down there."

"And if I do not agree?"

"You'll agree. I've got a gun, remember?"

"You would not shoot me in front of so many witnesses."

"No? I'm liable to do just about anything right now. Try me and see."

We matched stares for maybe thirty seconds. It was a will thing: he was trying to gauge whether or not his was stronger and he could make me back down. He must have decided that wasn't likely because he shrugged and said, "As you wish. Perhaps it is best that we do talk."

"When we go out, tell the kid at the door you're leaving for a few minutes. Use English so I know that's what you're saying. Make it casual; we're just a couple of guys going off to discuss business."

He dipped his head, came over to the door without hurry. I made a motion to the doorman, and the three of us went out into the parlor. Chuck repeated my words to the guard, who said something in Chinese; Chuck answered him in English, saying, "Yes, everything is fine." The guard seemed satisfied. Two-thirds of the men in the room followed us with their eyes as we filed out to the stairs, but none of them moved from their chairs. On the way down, I heard their conversation pick up and the renewed clatter of coins and tiles and chips. That was a good sign, but I stopped the three of us in the foyer for half a minute, just to make sure. Nobody appeared on the stairs.

Outside, Chuck unlocked the door to the herb shop and we went in. He led the way through the bead curtains at the rear, into a combination office and storage room. It contained a teak desk, and he sat down behind it and immediately rattled off half a dozen sentences in Chinese. The doorman moved over to a crate of some kind and sat on it and looked at the wall.

"I told him deafness is a virtue," Chuck said to me. "We can speak freely now."

"I've been speaking freely. It's your turn."

He made a steeple out of his hands and postured them against his lower lip. "Is it true that Jimmy Quon is dead?"

"It's true. I found him myself, a little more than an hour ago."

"At the temple of Tien Hou?"

"That's right. With his head bashed in."

"I do not like that," Chuck said. "A place of worship . . . such a crime is a sacrilege."

"Yeah," I said.

"How do you know Carl Emerson is responsible?"

"He hired Quon to kill Lieutenant Eberhardt; you already know that. What he's doing is burning his bridges. You understand what that means?"

"I am familiar with the expression."

"All right. Does Emerson know you know he hired Quon?"

"No."

"Where did you hear it? From Quon?"

"Yes."

"Did he tell you why?"

"Not specifically."

"Then as far as Emerson is concerned, Quon and one other person besides Eberhardt were the only ones who could link him to the shooting. He bought off the other person, but Quon was a different story."

"Who is this other person?"

"You don't need to know that. It's not important. The point is, Quon was making trouble because I pushed him into it. I suppose you know he tried to ambush me last night at my flat?"

"No, I did not know that."

"Well, he did. And Emerson didn't like it; he doesn't

know I'm on to him, and he was afraid I'd get Quon before Quon got me—afraid his name would come out into the open. Quon set up another ambush tonight; that was what he was doing at the temple. And what I was doing there, but I didn't know that until afterward. Emerson found out about it and went there and murdered Quon. You see?"

"Yes," he said. "I see."

I moved over to the desk, rested a hip against it. "Was Mau Yee anything to you? A close friend?"

"No. An acquaintance."

"But he was Chinese and he was a member of Hui Sip. You wouldn't want to see his killer get off free, would you? A Caucasian?"

"Perhaps not."

"Unless Emerson is a friend of yours. Is he?"

"No."

"So you tell me where I can find him and I'll take it from there. That way, we're both satisfied. Hui Sip, too."

"Do you intend to kill Mr. Emerson?"

"I don't know what I intend to do with him. I'll figure that out when the time comes."

"Perhaps you will decide to turn him over to the authorities."

"That's a possibility."

"If that were to happen, would you give them my name?"

"No. Not as long as you're cooperative."

"I would not like to be harassed by the police," he said.

"I'm not interested in you, Chuck. Now that Jimmy Quon is dead, the only person I'm interested in is Emerson."

I watched him think. At length he said, "Will you believe me if I tell you I do not know where you can find Mr. Emerson?"

"If it's the truth."

"It is. I do not know where he is. He lives in Burlingame; perhaps you should go to his home."

"I know where he lives. But there's a chance he might still be here in Chinatown. He didn't come around to the parlor tonight?"

"No. He did not."

"When was the last time you saw him?"

"Several days ago."

"Upstairs?"

"Yes."

"How often did he come here to gamble?"

"Once or twice a month." Chuck's mouth crooked sardonically. "He seldom lost. Mr. Emerson is quite a good poker player."

"Are you the one who introduced him to Jimmy Quon?"

"Not directly so. Jimmy worked for me on occasion. Mr. Emerson is generous with gratuities when he wins; they struck up an acquaintanceship."

"When did Quon tell you Emerson had hired him? Before the shooting or afterward?"

"Afterward. Jimmy was afflicted with a loose tongue."

"If you'd known about it beforehand, what would you have done?"

A small shrug. "Would you have me say I would have attempted to prevent it?"

"No," I said. The anger was plain in my voice; I wanted him to hear it. "You wouldn't have done anything. It wasn't any of your business, was it?"

"My business is herbs," he said. "And games of chance. I do not concern myself with the folly of others."

"Very practical. You're a sweetheart, you are."

"You may think of me what you wish. What you do about it is another matter."

"The same thing goes from my point of view," I said. "That's another reason why we're having this talk. Where do I stand with you and Hui Sip, now that Mau Yee is dead?"

He raised an eyebrow. "Do you fear tong vengeance?"

"Not fear it, no. But I'd like to know what to expect. If Hui Sip considers me an enemy, then I'll have to make it reciprocal. I'll have to go after them—and you—the same way I'm going after Emerson."

Chuck smiled faintly; it did not come anywhere near his eyes. "That would be most foolish. You could not hope to succeed."

"Maybe not, but I'd have to try. And I could probably make things pretty uncomfortable for you before it was over. Neither one of us wants that to happen. So how do I stand?"

"I cannot speak for Hui Sip. I can only speak as one of its elders."

"And?"

"I have no particular quarrel with you. Your difficulties here were with Jimmy Quon—a personal matter. I do not concern myself with personal matters any more than I concern myself with human folly."

"You think the other elders will feel the same way?"

"Possibly."

"You might want to talk to them about it," I said. "Just to keep the peace."

"I will consider it."

"You do that." I backed off from the desk. "This has been an interesting little chat. Wouldn't you say so, Chuck?"

"Most interesting."

I kept on backing until I reached the bead curtains. When I got there he said, "One final word before you leave. It is my wish that we shall never again have the pleasure of such a stimulating conversation. In view of that wish, my humble opinion is that you would be wise to avoid Chinatown in the future. Were I you, I would not even come here to eat in any of our excellent restaurants."

"I hear you," I said. "You leave me alone, I leave you alone. The next time I want Chinese food, I'll go somewhere out on the avenues."

"Then I wish you well in your search for Mr. Emerson. Good night, sir. And good-bye."

I backed through the curtains, across the shop to the entrance. Chuck and the doorman stayed where they were. When I opened the door my hand was shaking a little; I thought that it was a good thing I'd had it in my pocket the whole time, around the gun where Chuck couldn't see it.

Sometimes, like with the poker players upstairs, you can run a dangerous bluff and get away with it.

EIGHTEEN

IT WAS AFTER MIDNIGHT by the time I got to Burlingame, twenty-five miles south of the city, and found Camelia Drive. The street was two crooked blocks long, tucked back in a section that bordered on the even more affluent community of Hillsborough. The guy at the all-night service station on El Camino, where I stopped to ask directions, had never heard of it; I'd had to hunt up its location on a town map in his office.

The houses along Camelia Drive were smallish but expensive-looking, set on wide woodsy lots with plenty of space between them. Number Thirty-seven was partially hidden behind a tall hedge and a couple of big shade trees; illuminated numerals on the gate post let me place it from the car as I drifted by. There were no other lights that I could see, either in the house or in the detached garage.

I drove through a dogleg at the end of the block and parked under one of the trees that flanked the road, away from the hanging street lamps. But I did not get out right away. I was still as tense as I had been in Chinatown, but fatigue made me feel sluggish and achey; the coffee I'd bought from a vending machine at the service station didn't seem to have done much good. I rolled the window down, lay my head against the seatback, and sat there like that for a time.

When the chill air began to make me shiver I unclipped the flashlight from under the dash, put it into the coat pocket with the .38, and stepped out and headed back to Number Thirty-seven. It was heavily overcast here but with none of the fog that had blanketed San Francisco; the shadows under the trees were as black as ink on blotting paper. The only lights I could see came from street lamps, house numerals, and a single window in a house two hundred yards away, across the street.

I stopped at Emerson's front gate and peered through it at the house. Ranch-style, with a porch alcove made out of brick; dark and silent. I moved over to the driveway, went up it along the bordering hedge. There was just enough room between the hedge and the garage wall for me to squeeze through into the yard. A door with a glass pane was set into the wall toward the rear; I eased down there, walking on grass now, and put my face close to the glass. Solid black. I got the flashlight out and butted the lens against the window. When I flicked it on, for just a second, the flare of light showed me an empty expanse of oily concrete floor.

No car. No Emerson?

Following a flagstone path, I moved over toward the house and around onto the porch. There was a control plate for an alarm system in the wall next to the door, but the little bulb above the keylock was dark; unless it was burned out, that meant the system was not turned on. I tried the doorknob, being quiet about it, but it was locked up tight.

I went back onto the path, took the branch that led to the rear. More trees, a small flagstone terrace with some outdoor furniture on it, and a kidney-shaped swimming pool flanked by lawn on the other three sides. The same kind of tall hedges as out front separated Emerson's property from his neighbors' and gave it, and me, plenty of privacy.

In the near back wall of the house were a set of sliding glass doors; I stepped on to the terrace and tried them first. Locked. Beyond was a short wing containing a door in the inside angle, with a window beside it and two more windows in the outer wall. The wing door had a bolt lock and was set solidly in its frame. But the window near it was fastened by a loose-fitting latch, so that when I eased the sash upward with my fingers, it rose maybe a quarter of an inch before binding. With it up like that, there was a hair-line crack between the sash and the sill; I couldn't see it but I could feel it with my fingertips.

I took out my pocket knife, opened the longest of the blades, and poked it through the opening. It made faint scraping sounds when I wiggled it against the latch; I quit moving it to listen. Silence from inside the house. I did some more wiggling, making more noise now. But if Emerson was in there, and if he'd heard me, he was being damned quiet.

It took me a couple of minutes to wedge the latch out of its slot. Only it slipped right back in again because I couldn't hold it and slide the sash up at the same time, one-handed. I worked the latch free a second time, then leaned my chest against the knife handle and shoved at the sash with my hand. The same thing happened with the latch. I had to do it twice more, sweating, gritting my teeth, before I managed to hold the latch long enough to get the sash moving upward.

The thing made a grating noise when it went up, and the knife slid over the sill and clattered against something inside. I flattened against the wall with the .38 clear in my hand. Nothing happened in the house, but I stayed motionless for two or three minutes, listening hard, waiting. Still nothing, not even a creak.

All right, I thought. Nobody home. The son of a bitch isn't *that* good.

But I did not put the gun back into my pocket. I used it and the edge of my hand to shove the sash all the way up. Climbing in was another matter; I could have hauled myself over the sill if I'd had the use of both hands, but with just one it was impossible. I went over to the lawn furniture, picked up one of the wrought-iron chairs, and brought it back to the window. When I got up on that I was able to swing my leg inside. I straddled the sill, eased my head and the left side of my body under the sash, and managed to make it the rest of the way through without hurting myself.

Bulky shapes loomed in the darkness. I stayed where I was for half a dozen pulsebeats, listening to more silence; then I traded the gun for the flashlight and switched on the beam. An office or study. The bulky shapes were a desk, some cabinets and bookcases, three chairs, and a couch: all polished black teak bearing Chinese designs in gold leaf. The carpet was red and gold with a dragon motif. Even the pictures on the walls were Oriental, at least half of them erotic.

I found my knife and picked it up. An open doorway led into the main part of the house; I followed the light through it. On my right, a bead-curtained arch gave access to a recreation room, the one with the sliding glass doors. Straight ahead was a hallway, and the first door off it on the left led to the master bedroom. The flash beam let me see a canopied teak bed, black-lacquered nightstands and dressers with more gold-leaf designs, a Chinese tapestry on one wall—and it also let me see that some of the dresser drawers were pulled open, spilling out articles of clothing.

I went in there. Two or three other articles lay on the carpet; the gold-dragon bed quilt was mussed at the bottom, as if something heavy, like a suitcase, had lain there; inside a walk-in closet, a couple of suits and some shirts were pulled askew on their hangers and there were three empty hangers scattered on the floor. All of which could have meant that Emerson was the same kind of sloppy housekeeper as I was, except that the study and recreation room were neat and orderly. The other explanation, the obvious one, was that he had come back here tonight, packed in a hurry, and beat it away again.

Opposite the bed was a doorway that led to an adjoining

bathroom. When I played the light in there I saw a tan trench coat draped over the rim of the tub; one of its sleeves appeared to be damp. I moved inside for a closer look. The sleeve had been scrubbed with water and some kind of cleanser, probably not much more than an hour ago. And it had been a hurried job, because I could just make out the edges of several spotty stains that had not quite been washed out.

Blood, I thought, he got blood on the sleeve when he killed Jimmy Quon. He'd been here tonight, all right. But where the hell was he now?

I went back to the hallway and searched the rest of the house. All of the rooms had the same type of Oriental furniture and decor, even the kitchen, and all of them were as well kept as the study and the rec room. None contained anything that gave me a lead as to where Emerson might have gone.

Back in the study, I drew heavy brocade drapes over the windows and then switched on the desk lamp. An appointments calendar next to the phone bore several notations in a near-illegible hand; but there was nothing under today's date, and nothing under tomorrow's, and none of the scrawled names meant anything to me. I pawed through papers in the desk and in a teak file cabinet. Bills, personal and business records, a checking account statement that showed a balance of three thousand dollars. No private correspondence, and nothing to link Emerson to Eberhardt or Polly Soon or Jimmy Quon.

Once I was done in there, I had no reason to stay any longer. I shut off the lamp, climbed back out through the window, and closed it behind me. I left the lawn chair where it was, the hell with it. Camelia Drive was still deserted; I went out through the front gate and back to my car.

I sat in the darkness again, fighting off lassitude, trying to think. Where did he go? It figured he was badly upset, panicked; the hasty packing job proved that, and so did his

[163]

flight. But I could not see him going on the run. If he'd been inclined to run, he'd have done it when Eberhardt survived the shooting. And with Quon dead, and me apparently stymied, he had to believe he was more or less in the clear now. Then there was the trenchcoat. He'd washed it and left it in the bathroom, instead of getting rid of it; that had to mean he planned on returning home sooner or later.

A short trip, then. Get out of the area for a few days, hole up somewhere until he could pull himself together. It made sense that way. Hiring somebody to kill was one thing, but doing the job yourself was a whole different ball game. It took some getting used to, it kept a person from functioning in normal patterns.

Philip Bexley had told me Emerson made regular gambling trips to Las Vegas. Would he have hopped a plane and gone there? Maybe. But a much more likely possibility was the ranch in Mendocino County that Bexley had also told me about. Familiar surroundings on the one hand; a sense of isolation on the other. A place where he'd feel secure.

Mendocino or Vegas or some other damned place, there was nothing I could do about it tonight, no matter how much I wanted to pursue him. I was like a zombie already; if I did not get some rest pretty soon, I was liable to wind up back in the hospital. I couldn't do anything about Emerson from a frigging hospital bed.

It was a constant struggle to stay alert on the drive back to San Francisco. When I finally got home I was asleep on my feet. I don't even remember getting out of my clothes or crawling into bed.

In the morning, rested, still a little achey, I called Mid-Pacific Electronics. The woman who answered—the secretary, Miss Addison, probably—said, "I'm sorry, sir, Mr. Emerson isn't in," when I asked to speak to him.

"Will he be in later today?"

"No, he's gone out of town."

"For how long?"

"He won't be back until next Monday."

"Can you tell me where I can reach him?"

"I'm afraid not."

"He didn't happen to go to Las Vegas, did he?"

"Las Vegas? No, he didn't."

"Would he be up at his ranch in Mendocino?"

"I really can't say, sir. May I take a message?"

"No message," I said, and put the receiver down. And stood up and reached for my coat.

Yeah, I was thinking.

Mendocino.

Nineteen

I<small>T WAS RAINING</small> in Mendocino County.

I took Highway 101 straight up to Cloverdale, then cut
over on 128 through the orchards and vineyards of Ander-
son Valley, through towering redwood forests to the coast;
the rain started around Boonville, a thin misty drizzle. The
north coast of California gets a lot of rain, even in the
summer months—that, and a perpetual shroud of fog. By
the time I got to the village of Mendocino, the mixture of
fog and rain was so heavy you could barely see the ocean
lying beyond the headland.

The drive was a long one, better than five hours and a
hundred and fifty miles, and I was pretty tired at the end
of it. I had stopped twice, once in Santa Rosa for gas and
once in Cloverdale for coffee and a sandwich, but the stops
had not done much for me mentally or physically. My muscles were cramped, my back hurt, my shoulder hurt, I had
a tension headache. And I was in a wicked frame of mind:
wired up tight, with violence roiling just under the surface.
I was a little afraid of myself, of what I might do when I
finally came face to face with Carl Emerson. I could handle
it all right if he didn't make trouble, but if he provoked me
in any way . . . .

I quit thinking about that. If something was going to
happen, let it happen. Worrying about losing control could
make you do just that when you came up against it.

The village had been built on a rugged, tree-dotted

headland overlooking the mouth of the Big River and the sea beyond. It was the kind of place people called quaint, more New England than California in style and attitude—Cape Cod cottages, weathered Gothic buildings and towers, narrow streets lined with art galleries, coffee houses, shops dispensing a variety of local craftwork. A town populated by artists and artisans, most of them young, most of them dropouts from big cities like San Francisco. Mendocino was the heart of California's art renaissance, a haven for people who wanted a quieter, rural life-style without giving up a sense of culture and sophistication.

But the county wasn't all a bucolic utopia. Other kinds of dropouts had discovered it, too, back in the sixties; dope-dealing and marijuana-growing were two of its other thriving industries, and there were reputed to be training grounds for paramilitary and terrorist groups, right- and left-wing, in its more remote areas. Man builds and creates and lives in harmony with nature; man uses, tears down, turns beauty into ugliness, tranquillity into disorder. The age-old story, the biblical struggle between good and evil. A kind of Armageddon in microcosm, conducted in small daily skirmishes.

Armageddon for me, too, I thought. That was what I was here for, wasn't it? To finish my own personal battle with a force of evil?

I parked near the Masonic Hall, an old frame building with a rooftop sculpture of Father Time braiding a woman's hair, and dodged puddles and tourists with umbrellas until I found a shop that sold county topographical maps. I didn't expect to find Seaview Ranch listed on it, but I thought that maybe there was a Seaview Road or Seaview Lane in the vicinity of the village. There wasn't. So much for that idea.

Outside again, I hunted up a real estate office; if there was anybody who would know where Seaview Ranch was, it was a local realtor, particularly since the place had to have been on the market before Emerson bought it six months ago. The woman I talked to was in her fifties, smiling and cheerful despite the weather. I told her I was looking to buy a home in the area and that I'd heard a place called Seaview Ranch was up for sale. She was familiar with it, all right; without hesitation she said I was too late, that property had already been sold.

"That's too bad," I said. "Did you handle the transaction?"

"No, we didn't. It was another agency, in Fort Bragg."

"But you do know where Seaview Ranch is located?"

"Why, yes. I knew the former owner. I must say I was a bit disappointed that he didn't register the property with us when he decided to—"

"Would you mind telling me how to get to it?"

"Well . . . may I ask why you want to know?"

"From what I was told," I said, "it's exactly the sort of place I'm looking for. I'd like to take a look at it—talk to the new owner, see if he might be willing to sell if the price is right." I gave her a conspiratorial smile. "I'm pretty well off financially, so money is no object when I find something I want."

"I see." She hesitated, and then made a small shrug; it really didn't matter much to her one way or another. "Well, I suppose in that case . . . Seaview Ranch is about seven miles south of here, between Little River and Albion. It has a private road that branches off the highway, toward the ocean; you can't miss it because on one side there's a creek and on the other there's a hill with some rocks on it shaped like an arrow. The headland out there, where the ranch is, is called Arrow Point."

I thanked her, went back to the car, and drove south out of the village on Highway One. It was the same way I'd come in, because Highway 128 intersects One just below Albion; I had to have passed the access road to Seaview Ranch earlier. It was after five o'clock now, with a couple of hours of daylight left, but the rain and the fog had turned the day dark, strewn it with shadows. I was forced to turn on the headlights because of the poor visibility.

The highway clung to the edge of the coastline, dipping and twisting across wooded ridges and creek mouths, around deep coves with sea-sculpted walls and jumbles of wave-tunneled rocks, all obscured by the misty drizzle. A mile and a half past the hamlet of Little River, the landmarks I was looking for appeared on my right: the creek first, choked with underbrush and spanned by a short bridge, and then the road and the hill beyond. The rocks up there didn't look much like an arrow, but maybe that was because of the weather and the bad light: they had a way of distorting shapes, obliterating the contours of things.

I slowed and made the turn. There was a wooden gate closed across the road ahead, a sagging wood-and-wire fence stretching away on both sides. A sign on the gate said: *Private Property—No Trespassing.* I braked a few feet short of the gate, got out and went up to it. It was fastened by a wire ring looped over a short post; I unhooked the ring, shoved the gate open and swung it out of the way. The road, graveled, glistening with rain puddles in the headlight glare, curled to the left beyond and disappeared into the undulant wall of fog. Nothing else was visible except for a few trees and some craggy land studded with rocks, overgrown with bushes and coarse grass. The smell of the sea was sharp, brackish; I could hear the surf pounding away in the distance, muffled and rhythmic, a lonely sound.

When I got back into the car I took the .38 out of the glove compartment where I'd put it when I left San Francisco and laid it on the seat beside me. I could feel myself tightening up inside, little knots of pressure in my chest and groin. The tension and the contained anger made my mouth dry, the palms of my hands damp with sweat.

I switched off the headlights—if Emerson was here, I did not want him to know I was coming—and took the car through the open gateway. The road hooked around the edge of the hill, bent back to the right again past a stand of eucalyptus; the rest of the terrain stayed barren and rocky. I rolled down the window, driving at a crawl, so I could listen to the pound of the surf. It seemed closer now, a low booming pulse, as if the fog itself were a living thing.

More eucalyptus appeared ahead, and beyond them I could make out fuzzy clots of light and the vague shapes of buildings. The light meant he was here, all right. My right hand felt greasy as I eased the car up to where the trees were, stopped in their shadow, and shut the engine down.

With my fingers wrapped around the .38, I got out and moved forward along the edge of the road. The wind off the ocean was blustery, full of humming sighs and moans; it blew rain into my face, cold and stinging, like little pellets of ice. I paused alongside the last of the trees and wiped my eyes with my sleeve, squinting through the murkiness ahead.

The buildings were more distinct now, the nearest maybe seventy yards away on my right, across an open expanse of rumpled, grass-tufted ground. That one, weathered and gray and peak-roofed, had to be a barn; clustered near it were a couple of small outbuildings. Some distance removed to the left was the ranch house, an old-fashioned white frame structure, two-storied, sheltered by a half moon of wind-bent evergreens and eucalyptus. It was set at an angle so that it faced northwest, out toward the shoreline and the sea beyond. That was where the light was coming from: two windows in the front wall, one in the side wall facing me. A car, some sort of squarish compact, was drawn up near the porch.

I started across the open ground, angling toward the trees at the rear of the house. By the time I got there, I was wet and shivering. The back of the house was dark; I left the tree shadows and cut over to the near corner, moved along the side wall until I came to the lighted window. I put my back against the boards and craned my head forward to look through the rain-streaked glass. Front parlor, with the same Oriental motif as the Burlingame house; the Chinese furniture and rugs and tapestries looked incongruous in that Victorian room, out here in the middle of nowhere. The portion of the parlor that was visible appeared empty. I ducked under the window, flattened out on the other side, and took a look at the inner half.

A man was sitting half sprawled on a brocade couch near the fireplace, with his head lolling forward on his chest. He looked drunk; on the black-lacquered table in front of him was a nearly empty bottle of bourbon and an empty glass. But he wasn't Carl Emerson. I could see enough of his face to tell that, and to identify him.

Orin Tedescu.

I was past the point of being surprised by much of anything. I said, "Damn," under my breath, and went around to the front, up the stairs and onto the porch. When I turned the knob the door opened inward with a faint creaking sound. I shoved it wide, so I could see what lay within: a wide foyer, doorway to the parlor on the left, staircase at the rear flanked by a central hall, and another doorway on the right that opened into a darkened dining room. The only sounds came from outside—the crashing of surf, the steady drum of the rain.

I went in after a dozen seconds, eased the door shut, and stepped through into the parlor. Tedescu was still sitting in the same position, slack-mouthed, breathing through his nose in little snores that were inaudible until I got up close to him. His hair was damp, plastered down on his skull, as if he'd spent some time out in the rain; his shirt and trouser legs were also damp. And so was a tweed overcoat tossed over the arm of a nearby chair. The smell of liquor, mingled with that of wet fabric, came off him in waves. I poked him once with the muzzle of the .38, but he didn't respond. The way it looked, he had drunk himself into a stupor.

At the rear of the room was a closed door; I opened it and looked into an empty sitting room that had been turned into a study. I came back through the parlor, went across into the dining room and then into a kitchen at the rear. Empty. So were a screened rear porch, a big antiquated larder, and a bathroom with a wooden tank-type toilet.

I climbed the stairs to the second floor, taking it slow, holding the gun at arm's length. Three bedrooms, an upstairs sitting room, and another bathroom—all of them deserted. One of the bedrooms had an open suitcase on a rack, and the bed had been slept in. Emerson's suitcase, probably, which would mean that he'd spent the night here. But where was he now? And what the hell was Tedescu doing here?

Downstairs again, back into the parlor. Tedescu still hadn't moved. I put the .38 in my pocket, got a handful of his shirtfront, and shook him a couple of times. He grunted, made a feeble protesting gesture with one hand. I slapped him across the face, forehand and backhand, not being gentle about it. His head wobbled bonelessly, but his eyes stayed shut.

"Tedescu," I said, "wake up. Wake up!"

He muttered something, made a gagging noise as if he were going to vomit on himself. When I slapped him another time, his eyelids fluttered and finally popped up like window shades; he stirred and sat up. It took him a couple of seconds to get his eyes focused on me. They were blank at first, heavily bloodshot; then recognition, vague and fuddled, seeped into them. His mouth worked, but all that came out of it was spittle.

I sat on my heels in front of him. "Where's Emerson?"

Tedescu's lips twisted; he pawed at them with a shaky hand. Anguish, and maybe fear, glistened in his eyes. "Carl," he said in a thick slurred voice. "Jesus . . ."

"Where is he?"

"Gone," he said.

[172]

"Gone where?"

"Gone to hell, all gone to hell." He struggled forward, reaching for the bottle on the table, and managed to knock over an ashtray full of the stubs of his little cigars. I moved the bottle away from him, put it on the floor. "No," he said, "gimme that. . . ."

"Listen to me, Tedescu. Where did Emerson go?"

He threw his arm up in a vague gesture. "Out there. Ran out . . . crazy . . . went berserk . . ."

"Then what? Did he drive off?"

"No. Crazy . . ."

"You mean he's still around here somewhere?"

"Had that gun," Tedescu said. "Said he was gonna kill me, tried to . . . oh God!"

Whatever had happened, it was too much for him to cope with; it had driven him into alcoholic oblivion in the first place, and that was where he wanted to stay. After a couple of seconds his eyes rolled up in their sockets, the lids came down, and he flopped over on the couch, pulled his legs up, and sprawled onto his stomach. His breathing, harsh at first, settled into the faint snore. He was gone again.

I let him lie there. It would take time to bring him around enough so he could talk sense, and if Emerson was still here somewhere, maybe crazed and toting a gun, I had no time to waste. I hauled the .38 out and hurried back into the rain.

The yard area, as much of it as I could see, was stark and empty in the failing light. A worn path led away through the grass to the left, probably out to the end of the headland; but the shoreline and the sea beyond were invisible from here, lost in the drizzly mist. The ocean could not have been far away, though: I could hear the angry crash of waves breaking against rock.

I moved past the parked compact, across to where the barn loomed gray and spectral like something out of a Gothic movie. The ground in front was muddy, and there were rain-filled ruts in it leading up to the closed double doors. I slogged through the mud, pulled one of the door halves open. Inside, parked on the dusty wooden floor, was a new Lincoln Continental. Emerson's car, I thought; he must have driven it in here to get it out of the rain. And it had to mean he *was* still in the vicinity. It didn't make sense that he would have left the ranch on foot, in weather like this, when he could have driven instead.

Warily, I stepped inside. The barn smelled of dust and dampness and dry rot; no animals had been housed in it for a long time. Shadows clung to the rafters, to a barren hay-loft at the far end, to a workbench tacked onto the side wall. There was not much else in there except for cobwebs and some discarded pieces of furniture stacked near the bench. There wasn't anything to hear, either.

I opened the driver's door on the Continental. The dome light went on, letting me see that both the front and back seats were empty. I left the door open, because the light cut away some of the gloom, and moved toward the rear. But he wasn't back there, and he wasn't up in the loft; I climbed partway up the ladder to make sure.

Outside again, I crossed to the nearest of the outbuildings. Woodshed, filled with firewood and nothing else. The second structure, larger, more ramshackle, was a storage shed: wheelbarrow, a few rusting tools, a big steamer trunk. On impulse I opened the trunk. It was as empty as the rest of the shed.

Where is he? I thought.

Where the hell did he go?

I backed out of the shed, scanned the terrain again. No other buildings were visible; there wasn't anything except rock and grass and the few trees. Unless the path led to some sort of structure out at the edge of the headland . . . a boat house? That didn't seem likely. The coastline was rugged along here, and the winter storms that assaulted it were sometimes violent; a boat house that was not built out of concrete and anchored to the rock wouldn't last long against the onslaught of those hammering waves. But I was running out of places to look. And the path had to lead somewhere or it wouldn't be there.

The wind, gusting now, lashed me with icy rain that stung my eyes and blurred my vision; I had to keep wiping it away in order to see where I was going. My face was beginning to numb, and I had no feeling at all in the fingers of my left hand. I put my right hand into my coat pocket to keep it warm and the gun from getting too wet.

The ground began to slope downward, gradually, and the path angled between boulder-sized rocks and clumps of sawgrass. The thunder of the surf grew louder, until it seemed to be right in front of me. Then, through parting ribbons of fog, I could see the edge of the cliff ahead. The path went right up to it, over it, and out of sight.

When I got to where I could see beyond the edge I was looking down a steep incline to a jagged mass of rocks a good seventy feet below. The surf boiled over them, faintly luminescent—a wild, eerie sight that seemed to appear and disappear, phantomlike, in the mist. The path led all the way to the bottom, with rough steps cut into it at intervals. But not to any boat house. At low tide, there would probably be a slice of beach down there; now, the waves covered it, foaming partway up the cliffside. I could taste the salt spray they hurled up into the air when they broke.

I moved to my left, keeping well back from the edge. The rim of the headland bellied outward a few yards away; the incline straightened into a vertical rock wall. I retraced my steps, went across the path in the opposite direction. The terrain made a sharp inward turn over there. It extended back thirty or forty yards, then hooked outward again the same distance so that it formed a U-shaped cut maybe twenty yards wide. Below, the sea had fashioned a tiny cove halfway into the cut; the inner half was a sloping pile of eroded rock.

I started around the inner lip of the U. And then stopped

abruptly, because the mist parted again and I could see something down on those rocks, something blue billowing in the wind. I moved closer to the edge, pawing wetness out of my eyes, and knelt there on the muddy turf, hunched forward, peering down.

The blue thing was a jacket. And there was a man inside it, a man lying bent and twisted, caught between two of the rocks. The wind billowed his hair too, made it look like blond tendrils reaching up into the mist from the top of his shattered skull.

Jesus, I thought. Sweet Jesus.

I had finally found Carl Emerson.

TWENTY

I KNELT THERE, staring down at him, for more than a
minute. The tension leaked out of me, until there was
nothing left but a kind of inner numbness. I could not seem
to feel much. A small sense of relief, but that was all.

It was not supposed to end this way. It was supposed to
end in confrontation, maybe a fight, maybe death—but not
this kind of death. Ten days of hate, three days of finding
out who he was, tracking him down, building toward a final
showdown, and it had all come down to this: accident,
suicide, whatever. It had all come down to nothing.

I had never seen his face; I couldn't see it now in the rain
and fog. All he'd done to me and to Eberhardt, and I had
never laid eyes on him in person, or even spoken to him.
Never spoken to Jimmy Quon either, never saw *his* face
until he was just a broken lump of clay. So personal, and
yet not really personal at all.

Emerson, dead of a crushed skull. The same way he'd
ended Quon's life. The same way he'd ended Polly Soon's.
Irony in that. And more than irony, maybe—a kind of cos-
mic justice. Vengeance wasn't mine; Kerry had been right
about that. So had the Bible. Vengeance wasn't anybody's
on this earth.

I got to my feet, shivering, aware for the first time of how
tired I felt, of how much pain there was in me. I was still
hanging onto the .38, and when I looked at it I felt a sudden
revulsion. Black and ugly, an alien thing. That wasn't mine,

either. And I did not want it anymore, in my hand or in my pocket or anywhere near me. Milo Petrie would never understand, so I wouldn't bother to tell him. Not even when I paid him what he thought it was worth.

I reversed the gun in my fingers, so that I was holding it by the barrel, and hurled it away into the mist and the raging sea.

Orin Tedescu was still unconscious when I got back to the house. I took off my sodden overcoat, went into the downstairs bathroom, and used a towel to dry myself off. In the kitchen, I found a kettle and a big pitcher and filled both of them with water. The kettle I put on the gas stove to boil; the pitcher I carried into the parlor and dumped over Tedescu's head.

It brought him out of it. He sat up groggily, sputtering, and gave me a blank look. He had forgotten about our little scene earlier; I watched him recognize me all over again with the same befuddlement. A belch came out of him, then a low moaning noise. He started to fumble around for the bourbon bottle.

I said, "Uh-uh," and hoisted him to his feet and marched him out into the kitchen. He had trouble walking and I had to hang on to his arm; but he came along all right, without struggling. I sat him down at the table, gave his head a rough rubdown with the towel I'd used on myself. When I was done with that he sat slumped forward, gray and sick-looking, supporting his head between the heels of his hands.

The water in the kettle started to boil. I hunted up a jar of instant coffee and a couple of mugs, made the coffee, and put one of the mugs down in front of him. "Drink that," I said.

He stared at it. "No. Don't want it."

"You're going to sober up one way or another. You want

me to take you upstairs and throw you in the shower?"

"No."

"Then drink the goddamn coffee."

He drank it. He tried to pick up the mug at first, but his hands were too shaky; he had to lean forward and sip from it where it sat. I finished what was in my own mug, and that warmed me a little, got rid of the shivering. Then I made second cups for both of us.

Tedescu said, "Jesus!" in an anguished voice, and when I turned around he was staring at the tabletop with the anguish all over his face. Some of the liquor haze had cleared out of his head and he was remembering again what had happened between him and Emerson. "Carl . . ."

"He's dead," I said.

"Dead . . ." He squinted at me. "How you know?"

"I saw him out there on the rocks."

"Accident," he said thickly. "Swear it was. *Swear* it!"

I pushed the fresh mug under his nose. "Keep drinking the coffee. You're not sober enough to talk yet."

"No more. Need another drink . . ."

"Forget that. Do what I told you."

He didn't give me any more argument; he seemed to be the kind of man who was used to obeying orders. As soon as he finished the second cup, I fed him a third. He gagged a couple of times, but he got all of it down and kept it down. He had the habitual drinker's strong stomach, and the habitual drinker's ability to sober up in a fairly short time. The third cup of coffee did it; his eyes lost some of their confusion, if none of their anguish, and he said in a steadier, less slurred voice, "Christ, why didn't you leave me alone. Why didn't you let me stay drunk?"

"I want to know what happened here today. You're the only one who can tell me."

He grimaced. "Don't want to talk about it."

"Maybe not, but you're going to."

I sat down across from him. He squinted at me again,

over the top of his mug. "You're James," he said. "Andrew James?"

"That's right."

"Don't understand. Why're you here, way up here?"

"I came to talk to Emerson."

"Why?"

"Personal reasons. Now suppose you tell me why *you're* here?"

"Business. Contracts had to be signed."

"What contracts?"

"Important contracts. Told him that when he called."

"He called you? When?"

"Last night, late. Said he was going to Mendocino for few days, didn't want to be bothered for any reason; said Phil Bexley and I should handle things at the office. Tried to tell him about contracts, but he wouldn't listen. Sounded strung out."

"So you went in to Mid-Pacific this morning and got the contracts and drove up here with them. Is that it?"

"Yes. No choice. Somebody had to do it."

"What happened when you got here?"

Another grimace. "He'd been drinking. Looked half-wild . . . Christ, never saw him like that before."

"How did he act?"

"Crazy . . . like a crazy man. Yelled at me, called me names. Wouldn't sign contracts. Told me to go away, leave him alone."

"Then what?"

"Tried to reason with him, make him understand how important contracts were. But he shoved me, knocked me down. No warning . . . just shoved me, knocked me down."

"What did you do?"

"Got up and hit him," Tedescu said. A look of awe crossed his bleary features, as if he could not believe he had done anything like that. "Never liked Carl, never got along with him . . . always wanted to hit him. This time I did it. Knocked *him* down, by God."

"Did he retaliate?"

"No. Screamed at me, told me get the hell off his property. Then he ran out."

"Why?"

"Don't know. I think"—the awed look again—"think he was afraid he might kill me."

"Why do you think that?"

"He had a gun. Big gun . . . Jesus, a cannon."

One of Jimmy Quon's puppies, I thought, the one Emerson had taken off Quon's body after he killed him. I said, "You mean he pulled the gun on you before he ran out?"

"No. Later, on the cliff."

"Is that where he ran off to?"

"Yes."

"And you went after him. Why?"

"Not sure. I was confused. Thought I could calm him down, apologize for hitting him, smooth it over. If I hadn't chased him . . ." Tedescu shook his head. Sweat glistened on his face, made the ruptured blood vessels look like fresh wounds.

"What happened on the cliff?"

"He was just standing there, looking down at ocean," Tedescu said. "But when he heard me coming . . . he went berserk. Pulled gun out of his jacket, kept yelling he was going to shoot me. Never been scared like I was then—never."

"So you jumped him," I said.

"What else could I do? Didn't even think, just . . . ran at him. Hit him with my shoulder and he lost his footing . . . went over . . . I knew he was dead soon as I saw him down there. . . ."

"What about the gun? Did that go over too?"

"Yes. Caromed off rock into the sea." Tedescu's eyes

were imploring now. "An accident, you see? Self-defense. I didn't mean for him to die, swear I didn't. . . ."

"All right," I said.

"You believe me, don't you?"

"I believe you."

I got up and went over to stand by the sink, looking out at the gray rain. I still was not feeling much. Just tired—scooped out inside.

Behind me, Tedescu said miserably, "What makes man like Carl start carrying a gun? What makes him go berserk all of a sudden?"

"I don't know," I said, but I did know. Guilt, depression, a feeling of persecution. Polly Soon's death had been an accident, or at least unpremeditated, and he'd been able to deal with that, rationalize it; he'd been able to deal with having Eberhardt shot, too, because he wasn't pulling the trigger himself. But Jimmy Quon's murder, the one he'd done with his own hands, had broken him down. That was why he'd come up here last night, and all the lonely hours before Tedescu's arrival had intensified the breakdown. So had the drinking, probably. He was on the ragged edge when Tedescu showed up, and the scuffle in here had pushed him over, just as the scuffle on the headland had pushed him over that other edge to his death.

I turned from the window. Tedescu was trying to light one of his cigars with shaking fingers; it took two matches before he got it going. "What do we do now?" he said. "Call the authorities?"

"Do you want to talk to them?"

"God, no. I couldn't call them after it happened; tried but I couldn't. Booze . . . that's all I could do."

"I don't want to talk to them, either," I said. Because it would mean explaining why I was here, bringing the whole thing with Eberhardt and Jimmy Quon and Polly Soon out into the open. And I was not ready to do that yet. Maybe I would never be ready to do it. "Emerson's death was an accident. There's no point in either of us going through a police interrogation."

He looked relieved. But it didn't chase away the anguish in his eyes; that, and the memory of what had happened here today, would stay with him a long time. "But what about Carl's body? We can't just leave it out there."

"No. How many people know you came up here today?"

"Only our secretary, Miss Addison. Contracts delivered to her this morning; she had them on her desk when I got to office."

"Okay. I'll take the phone off the hook before we leave. When you get back to the city, tell Miss Addison that Emerson wasn't home when you got here. You waited around but he didn't show up. Have her try to call him; she'll keep getting a busy signal. Tell her you're worried about Emerson and get her to call the county sheriff's office. They'll find the body when they come out to check. Can you handle it that way?"

"Think so. Yes."

"You're in no condition to drive back tonight," I said. "Neither am I, for that matter. We'll go put up at a motel; then I'll bring you back here in the morning to pick up your car."

He gave me a long, bewildered look. "Why you want to help me like this? Don't understand that. Who are you?"

"Andrew James," I said.

"Yes, but . . . did you know Carl?"

"No, I never met him. And I'm glad I didn't; it wouldn't have been a good thing for me."

"But you came here to see him. You said personal reasons . . ."

"It doesn't matter now. He's dead; my business with him is finished. Yours, too. Maybe things will be better for Mid-Pacific with him gone."

"Maybe will," Tedescu said. "He was a bastard. Not sorry he's dead, you know? Only sorry I had to . . ." He shuddered, wiped a hand across his face as if wiping away guilt. "You're right," he said, "over and done with. Carl's dead. You and me, we have to go on living."

I nodded. But as I started to clean up the kitchen, I thought that it wasn't over and done with, not quite, not as far as I was concerned. There were still two important matters to be resolved.

There was still Eberhardt.

And there was still the bribe.

TWENTY-ONE

I GOT BACK to San Francisco late Thursday afternoon. Tedescu didn't follow me down. The last I saw of him was in Albion; he trailed me there, after I took him back to Seaview Ranch to pick up his compact, and then pulled off in front of a grocery store. After liquor or beer, probably, something to take the edge off his hangover. He was pretty shaky, subdued; he'd had a bad night. But he'd get through all right, if he didn't start drinking heavily again and kill himself on the highway. The booze was his crutch —he'd been leaning on it for years and he would not stop leaning on it now. The irony was, Emerson had screwed up Tedescu's life when he was alive, and even in death he was still screwing it up. Tedescu might never get over what Emerson had done to him, what Emerson had caused him to do. And maybe I would never get over what Emerson had done to me, either.

I'd had a better night than Tedescu, but not by much. Dreams, fever sweats, nagging pain that kept bringing me up to the edge of consciousness. And all the running around in the rain had given me a head cold on top of everything else; it started after I had checked us into the motel—one room, twin beds, so I could keep an eye on Tedescu—and when I woke up I was snuffling and I had a scratchy throat. All of me ached; Doctor Abrams' warning about pneumonia was in the back of my mind. I managed the long drive all right, but I was exhausted again when I finally got home.

I took some cold capsules and Vitamin C and went straight to bed. And slept sixteen hours, most of them dreamless. When I awoke on Friday morning I was still stiff and sore, and I still had the cold, but I felt somewhat better. I got up long enough to eat, went back to bed, and called Abrams at S.F. General to check on Eberhardt. No change. Then I dialed the Hall of Justice and got through to Ben Klein. I had to know how things stood with the police investigation, what the official position was on the death of Mau Yee.

But I had no worries there. "Still nothing definite to report," Klein said. "Trying to get answers in Chinatown is like trying to pry open an oyster shell with your fingers. Hear no evil, see no evil, speak no evil."

"No new leads?"

"One possibility, maybe, but I don't think it's going to get us anywhere. Chinese thug named Jimmy Quon got himself killed on Wednesday night. One of the body-washers we checked out after the shooting—a real hard case. But he had an alibi we couldn't shake."

"You think his death might be connected?"

"If it is, we can't find the connection. Found in an alley off Waverly Place, skull bashed in. No witnesses, no leads. It could be a gang killing; that kind of shit goes down all the time in Chinatown."

Found in an alley, I thought. Lee Chuck must have sent some Hui Sip people over to the temple to remove the body, probably because he didn't want cops, Caucasian cops, doing any more desecrating of a house of worship. How somebody like Chuck could have religious feelings was beyond me. But then, there seemed to be a lot of things that were beyond me these days.

I slept another three hours, doctored myself with more pills, ate again, and then screwed up my courage and called

Kerry at the Bates and Carpenter agency. Her secretary took the call, said she'd see if Ms. Wade was still in, and left me hanging for two minutes. Or Kerry did. Then the line clicked and Kerry's voice said, "Well—so you're still alive." She sounded cool and distant, but I thought I could detect relief, too. "I was beginning to think you'd disappeared for good. Or that you'd turn up dead in an alley somewhere."

"Have you been trying to call me?"

"Twice. Don't ask me why."

"I know why. At least, I hope I do."

No response.

"Listen," I said, "it's been a crazy time. I was a little crazy myself for a while. But that's over now. No more running around, no more guns."

Pause. "Is that the truth?"

"It's the truth."

"What happened? Did you find out who did the shooting? Did you finish your vendetta?"

"I finished it, but it wasn't a vendetta. I didn't kill anybody, if that's what you think. No violence."

"I suppose you still don't want to talk about it."

"Someday, maybe. Not yet."

Another pause. "So where are you now?"

"Home in bed, taking care of myself. It's where I'll be all weekend. Come over tomorrow or Sunday and see for yourself. I'd ask you to come tonight, but I'm still catching up on my sleep."

"I don't know if I want to see you."

"I'm not a stranger anymore, Kerry. Maybe not the person I used to be, but not a stranger. Come on over tomorrow and we'll talk; you'll see."

"I might be busy," she said. "I just don't know yet."

She came at one o'clock on Saturday afternoon. I thought she would, but I was relieved when the doorbell rang and I heard her voice over the intercom from downstairs. More sleep and the antibiotics had got rid of my cold; my shoulder was better too. Only the stiffness in my arm seemed as bad as it had been before.

There was still some distance between us, but it was tolerable. We talked, and she fixed me some lunch and changed the sheets on the bed, and when she left at four she kissed me. I said, "I'll call you pretty soon," and she said, "Or I'll call you." All in all, it was a promising time.

She had brought me the morning paper, and after she was gone I took it back to bed and read through it. On an inside page there was a short article that said Carl Emerson, a prominent local businessman, had been found dead at his Mendocino ranch by sheriff's deputies investigating a call from business associates who had been unable to reach him. The cause of death, according to the Mendocino County coroner, was an accidental fall.

On Sunday, Jeanne Emerson called. She'd also seen the article in the paper, and the first thing she said to me was, "Did Carl really die in an accident?"

"As far as I know, yes."

"It wouldn't matter if it was something else. I was just wondering. Was he involved in the shooting, as you thought?"

"I guess he was. But it's finished now, as far as I'm concerned; how about if we just leave it that way?"

"Whatever you say," she said. "I'm not sorry he's dead, though."

"Neither am I."

"About that photojournalism piece on you I suggested—I'd still like to do it, if you're willing."

"One of these days, maybe. Not right now."

"I'll call you in a few weeks, then. All right?"

"All right," I said.

On Monday, I went in to see Doctor Abrams. The wound in my shoulder was healing satisfactorily now, he said, and I seemed to be in reasonably good health. The continuing stiffness in my arm and hand was another matter. He said that therapy might correct the problem and that I ought to consult a specialist. If therapy didn't do it, I might have to have an operation.

I did not have to ask him what would happen if an operation didn't do it either.

And on Wednesday, after seventeen days in a coma, Eberhardt finally regained consciousness.

I knew he would sooner or later—there had never been any question in my mind—but it was a relief when Ben Klein called late that afternoon to tell me the news. I said, "How is he? Coherent?"

"Yeah, thank God."

"No memory damage?"

"None. He remembers everything that happened."

"Then you've talked to him?"

"Just for a couple of minutes, about an hour ago."

"What did he say?"

"Not much. Asked if we found who did the shooting, if we had any idea why. I hated to have to tell him no."

"Is that all he said?"

"Well, he asked about you. Wants to see you whenever the doctors'll allow it. Tomorrow sometime, probably."

I rang up S.F. General early Thursday morning and got through to Abrams. He said I could come in at eleven. I was there at ten-thirty, pacing up and down in the visitor's waiting area, trying not to think about what was coming. I just wanted to get it over with.

They let me go in right at eleven. It was a private room,

and Eberhardt was lying cranked up in the bed with his head swathed in bandages. A tube led down out of a suspended bottle into another bandage on his arm; they were still feeding him intravenously. He looked shrunken and gray and old—old.

I pulled one of the metal chairs over next to the bed and sat down. He said in somebody else's voice, wan and thin, "Don't ask me how I feel. I feel lousy."

"You'll get better."

"Yeah. So they tell me. How's your arm?"

"Not too bad. Still need the sling, though."

"You going to have full use of it?"

"Sure. Never mind about my arm. You just came out of two and a half weeks in a coma."

"Been better if I'd never come out of it at all," he said. "If it wasn't for me, you'd never have got shot."

"I know," I said.

"You know? What do you know?"

"All of it, Eb. Who shot us, who hired it done. And why."

The room seemed to get very still. Pain flickered across his face, and guilt, and remorse. He could not look at me anymore; he averted his eyes. It was several seconds before he spoke again.

"How did you find out?"

"Kam Fong called me after I got home from the hospital," I said. "He gave me a name—Mau Yee, a Chinese body-washer—and said the shooting had to do with some kind of bribe. I went to your place and opened your safe and found the stock-transfer form. The rest of it was detective work."

"You always were a hell of a detective," he said. "Why didn't you tell the Department?"

"Because I didn't believe it at first. Because I'd been shot too and I was angry and I wanted to know the truth."

"And now you do."

"Now I do."

"This Mau Yee . . . is he still on the loose?"

"No. He's dead. Carl Emerson killed him."

A tic started up on the left side of his face; it took him a few seconds to get it under control. "Why did Emerson kill him?"

I told him why. I told him all of it, straight through to my abduction of Lee Chuck from his gambling parlor; how I'd found out about Emerson, how I'd pieced the whole thing together.

He said, "You crazy bastard. You could have got yourself killed, messing with a Chinatown tong."

"But that didn't happen. I'm still here."

"And Emerson? What did you do about him?"

"I didn't do anything about him. He's dead, too."

"Christ. How?"

I explained that, omitting Tedescu's name; I just said it was somebody who knew Emerson who'd been the catalyst in his accidental death.

"So nobody's left," Eberhardt said, "nobody knows the full story except you and me. And you still didn't go to the Department."

"I was waiting to talk to you," I said.

"Suppose I hadn't come out of it. Then what?"

"I never doubted that you'd come out of it."

"But if I hadn't?"

"I don't know. I guess I wouldn't have done anything."

"Why not? Why shield a cop you figure's gone dirty?"

"Did you go dirty, Eb?"

Silence for a time. Then he said, "You think I been taking all along? One of the graft boys?"

"No," I said.

"Well, you're right. I never took anything in thirty years —not a nickel, not even a cup of coffee. Tempted a couple of times; who doesn't get tempted? But I never gave in. I didn't think it was in me to give in. . . . "

He fell silent again. I waited. He was getting around to

it; it was something he had to tell in his own way, maybe the hardest thing he'd ever had to tell anybody.

"But things happen," he said. "Some things you prepare for, like you get old and you get tired. Some things you don't prepare for, because you never figure they can happen. Like your wife walking out on you, taking up with some other guy. Taking the guts right out of your life. You understand what that can do to a man?"

"Yeah," I said, "I understand."

"Maybe you do. You wake up one morning, you're fifty-three years old, you're all alone, you got bills up the ass and half the money you thought you had in the bank is gone because the bitch grabbed off her share when she walked out. You say to yourself: I got to hang on, it'll all work out. So you hang on. What the hell else can you do?"

He might have been talking about me, too. Substitute losing your profession for losing your wife, and there wasn't much difference between us. Or there hadn't been up until three weeks ago. The difference now was that I was still hanging on and he'd already let go.

"But then maybe you get tempted again," he said, "one day right out of the blue. Not small potatoes this time, a whole goddamn feast. And all you got to do is look the other way on something nobody gives a damn about anyway. You get mad, you say no at first—but maybe you keep on listening. And maybe you break open inside and for a little while you stop caring. And maybe the no turns into a yes."

"I guess I can understand that, too," I said. "But it was a homicide case, Eb. I don't understand how you could look the other way on a homicide."

His cheek began to tick again. "It wasn't murder," he said. "Emerson swore up and down Polly Soon's death was an accident. The witness, Ming Toy, corroborated it; she saw the two of them scuffling, the Soon woman tripped and went off the walkway, that was all there was to it."

"Why were they scuffling?"

"Argument over how much she was charging him. He lost his temper and smacked her; she tried to claw him. Manslaughter, that was all I had on him. A smart lawyer could have got him off with a suspended sentence."

"Did you tell Emerson that?"

"I told him. But he said the publicity would ruin him. His company was about to go public; he stood to lose millions."

"And that was when he made his pitch."

"Yeah. One thousand shares of Mid-Pacific stock, transferred over to me. Worth six figures in a few years, he said. Better than cash—security for the future. Pay taxes on the income, everything on the up and up; no way for either of us to get caught."

"So you took it."

"I took it." He lifted a hand and rubbed the knuckles across his mouth. "You think I'm a real shit, don't you?"

"I'm not here to pass judgment on you, Eb."

"You don't have to; I've already done that. But it's not as cut and dried as it seems. I took the stock-transfer and went home and put it in my safe. But I didn't sleep that night and I didn't go to the Hall the next day. I kept thinking about it, all the clean years thrown away. And it got to me. I couldn't go through with it. You can believe that or not, but it's the truth."

"I believe you," I said.

"I called Emerson that Friday and told him I'd changed my mind. I told him I'd give him until Monday noon to turn himself in; otherwise I'd have to go after him. I told him if he said anything about the bribe offer, I'd deny it and it would go twice as bad for him."

"What did he say?"

"I didn't give him time to say much of anything. I thought I had him buffaloed." He made a sound that might have been a bitter laugh. "Some cop I am, huh? I underestimated that son of a bitch by a mile."

I said, "What about the stock-transfer form? What did you say you'd done with that?"

"Destroyed it. I guess he believed me; if he'd thought I still had it, he probably wouldn't have tried to have me blown away."

"Why didn't you destroy it?"

"I was going to." He paused. "I think I was going to."

"But you're not sure."

"No," he said, "I'm not sure. I took it out of the safe half a dozen times on Saturday and Sunday, to get rid of it, but I always put it back. I guess I was giving myself until Monday morning to make a decision."

"What would you have done on Monday?"

"I don't know. Either destroyed the form or called Emerson back and told him I was going through with it after all." He closed his eyes; the pain, the uncertainty, lay over his features like a mask. "I don't know," he said.

Both of us were quiet for maybe a minute. I finally got up and went to the one window and stood there looking out. Without turning, I said, "What happens now, Eb?"

"That's up to you, isn't it? You got the form."

"It's not up to me, it's up to you. Your decision."

"Suppose I decide to just sweep it under the rug, go on as if nothing happened? Promise you I'd never do anything like this again? Would you go along with it?"

"Probably. We've been friends a long time."

"But we wouldn't be friends anymore."

"No," I said. "Not anymore."

Silence again. At length he said, "If I make a clean breast of it, they'll put me up on charges and take away my pension."

"Maybe not. Your record's too clean."

"That doesn't count for much these days. Everything's

public relations, the squeaky clean image; you ought to know that if anybody does."

I didn't say anything.

"The least they'd do is suspend me without pay," he said. "How the hell would I live?"

"You'd find a way. Just like I'm going to do."

"There'd be an investigation and they'd find out about you; there wouldn't be any way to keep you clear. Practicing without a license, withholding evidence, breaking and entering, failure to report a homicide . . . you could go to jail."

"I don't care about that."

"No? Well I do."

I turned and looked at him again. He was staring up at the ceiling; his eyes had a haunted look.

"The other thing I could do," he said, "I could take an early retirement. Voluntary. Claim mental disability. That way, I'd get my pension." He ran his tongue over dry lips. "I earned my pension, goddamn it. I was a good cop for a lot of years."

"One of the best."

"Okay. Give me a little time to think it through, will you? Twenty-four hours?"

"Sure," I said. "Take all the time you want."

"You better get out of here now. I don't feel like talking anymore."

"All right. I'll come back tomorrow."

"I'll be here," he said. "I'm not going anywhere."

When I got home I took the stock-transfer thing out of the nightstand drawer where I'd put it, carried it into the bathroom, tore it into pieces and flushed the pieces down the toilet. No matter what Eberhardt decided, that paper was a symbol of ugliness—the last tie to Carl Emerson, the last tie to corruption and murder and all the craziness of the past three weeks. Getting rid of it was like purging myself of the last vestiges of a disease.

Then I called Kerry and invited her to come over and have dinner with me.

Then I got on with the business of living my life.

FREE!!
BOOKS BY MAIL
CATALOGUE

BOOKS BY MAIL will share with you our current bestselling books as well as hard to find specialty titles in areas that will match your interests. You will be updated on what's new in books at no cost to you. Just fill in the coupon below and discover the convenience of having books delivered to your home.

PLEASE ADD $1.00 TO COVER THE COST OF POSTAGE & HANDLING.

BOOKS BY MAIL

320 Steelcase Road E.,
Markham, Ontario L3R 2M1

210 5th Ave., 7th Floor
New York, N.Y., 10010

Please send Books By Mail catalogue to:

Name _____
(please print)

Address _____

City _____

Prov./State _____ P.C./Zip _____

(BBM1)